C J AXLEROD

DOUBLE

DOWN

ISBNs:
Paperback: 978-1-80227-230-7
eBook: 978-1-80227-231-4

Dark Words Publishing,
Shepherds Green,
Oxfordshire.
darkwordspublishing@gmail.com

Contents

1

CHAPTER

All Brian could feel was hate.

Pure, destructive, vengeful hate.

He had watched his best friend, Dave Finch, or should he say his ex-best friend, ask Karen Spalding if she wanted to sit and have lunch together.

David knew he shouldn't have even spoken to her.

Karen was his and only his. Brian had told David that a thousand times, yet the moment his back was turned, the little creep asked Karen to sit with him at lunch. What was worse—way worse—was that she'd said yes.

David knew full well that Brian had been working up the nerve to ask Karen to go out with him. Yet, not only did he make a move during lunch, but a few days later, Brian had seen them kissing behind the sciences building.

As far as Brian was concerned, that was the final straw.

David could have salvaged their friendship If he'd only remembered that Karen was Brian's girl. David had only to have backed out of the lunch engagement and all would have been forgiven.

Brian wasn't a monster. He understood the power of Karen's crystal blue eyes and delicate freckles that could make one forget all of life's other priorities. But David hadn't backed out, and what was worse—far worse—was that he'd seen David boasting about the kiss with Karen to some of the other kids in their class.

There was no forgiveness after knowingly stabbing your best friend in the back. At least, not in Brian's rule book.

In his book, you only ever got one chance.

They stood under the bus stop overhang at the side of Tamiami Trail North, trying to avoid the mid-afternoon downpour that was part of the hell that was Southern Florida in the summer. Anywhere else in America, a major downpour would freshen the air and usually even lower the temperature. Not in South Florida where a biblical downpour amidst a violent thunderstorm always managed to leave the town hotter than before the rain. The humidity went up instead of down and the whole place just became sticky.

David had tried a few times to get his friend talking, but Brian wouldn't respond and just kept staring out into the deluge.

"Come on, man. What did I do?" David asked.

"You know perfectly well what you did," he seethed.

"You're not still hung up over Karen asking to sit with me at lunch, are you? That's bullshit. I just wanted to talk to her about the history essay we've been assigned. I want some help deciding what period to write about."

"You could have asked me," Brian stated.

"No, I couldn't," David answered. "You suck at history."

"You betrayed me," Brian said in barely more than a whisper. "Friends don't betray each other."

"Whoa! Betray? What the hell?! What's all this betray crap? I just said I'd have lunch with her. Nothing else…just lunch. You've really got to lighten up about Karen. She already thinks you're too intense and a little creepy. What you need to do is to stop coming off so weird, just 'cause you like someone."

The storm managed to find one last kiloton of power. Fork lightning sizzled across the grey sky, followed less than a second later by a thunderous explosion that shook the ground. The blast caused David to jump as he stood with his back to the street and faced his friend.

"Wow! That was amazing," David gasped, then grinned like an idiot.

Brian smiled back at David and saw a dump truck approaching in his peripheral view.

David finally stopped grinning when Brian gave him a hard shove and he began to fall backwards towards the street. David's arms started flailing at nothing but air as a scream rose in his throat.

The truck was doing over sixty when it hit him.

Brian watched David basically explode as the twenty-five ton, fully loaded truck collided with his young body. One moment he looked like David, the next second he was just a burst bag of blood. It took the driver a couple of hundred yards to stop.

Even while he managed to bring his truck under control and steer it to the side of the road, his windscreen wipers were still spreading the gore back and forth in sweeping arcs.

2

CHAPTER

Alex Cole sat in the back of the Range Rover re-reading the latest rewrite on *Hell After Dark*. This was the twelfth draft, and he still wasn't feeling it. They still had a few months until principal photography started, but he was worried that the studio was losing the message of the story by bringing in one writer after another. Alex wasn't just starring in the film; he also had the contractual ability to nix any script that he felt wasn't ready to be shot.

Alex wielded a lot of power in Hollywood. Twenty-four years earlier, he had become an instant teen heartthrob in his first professional role. The part of Jake Fallon, in the soap *Days and Nights*, garnered him a daytime Emmy and the attention of many a casting director. Alex had never looked back. He was now one of the highest-paid performers in the world and with eighty percent of his films grossing over a quarter of a billion dollars, he was worth every penny to those who held a financial interest.

Alex was taking a risk with *Hell After Dark*. He had so far focused solely on the action-adventure genre and always played the part of the guy who was never meant to be the hero, but somehow, just was.

Hell After Dark was a complete dichotomy. For the first time, Alex was going to play the villain in a film directed by his best friend and actor, Codi Walsh. He was to portray a demonic archangel who had been sent to collect a long-overdue soul. Alex hadn't been that excited about the role when he read the first draft of the script, but Codi had persuaded him to read the novel instead.

Alex couldn't put it down. It was terrifying, while, at the same time, it had a deeply moral sub-tone. He agreed to star in the film version but both he and Codi were getting more worried by the day that the producers couldn't seem to get the script to match the tone of the book. The latest draft read like a bad, low-budget horror movie.

Alex had asked the studio head, Martha Hess, to have lunch with him and Codi at the Ivy in West Hollywood. They wanted to get Martha away from the secure walls of Magnum Pictures, thereby removing her home-field advantage. They planned to double-team her into agreeing to a completely new draft from a writer who wasn't part of the Magnum stable. They'd given twelve different writers a shot and it was time to step away from the 'approved scribes' and give someone with a fresh approach a chance to write the script. They both wanted Alicia Rhone to write a draft. She had, after all, written the book, but with no previous film script experience, the studio had been uncomfortable with the idea of backing a first-time script writer.

Alex looked out of the tinted windows and marvelled at the manicured gardens that abutted Santa Monica Blvd as they neared West Hollywood. He couldn't remember ever seeing anyone trimming or mowing the area and yet the narrow city park was always pristinely groomed.

He smiled at his own parallel image. Alex, too, was never seen in person without looking the part of a perfectly groomed film star; immaculate, stylish and fit. People lined up to see the Alex Cole they knew from the big screen. He didn't want that fragile love affair to be broken by something as avoidable as TMZ obtaining a photo of him looking unshaven and slovenly, not that that was likely to happen. Alex took his good looks very seriously. He ate well, exercised daily, did yoga and drank alcohol with as much moderation as possible.

In low light, Alex still looked as he had in his first movie over twenty years earlier. His six-foot frame was still lean, his blue eyes were as sharp as ever and his sandy blond hair hadn't dared to recede. Alex knew he was basically no more than a commodity, and, as such, could be replaced at any time with a newer, shinier version.

That was one of the main reasons why he wanted, if not needed, *Hell After Dark* to be a success. Despite his continued popularity, Alex knew that playing the older but still youthful and dashing version of his younger self, had to be getting close to its sell-by date. He needed to break the mould and recreate himself into someone who could connect with audiences of all ages even as he himself ripened into a more mature performer.

It wasn't that he feared getting older. He was just terrified of appearing to be fighting the natural process of ageing, especially if it was only so that he could continue giving the same performance in the same genre until it finally became a joke to everyone but himself. Many A-listers were fighting that same battle, especially those who had stayed solely in the action realm. Though pleasantly nostalgic for the audience, nobody was going to continue to pay to see a seventy-year-old actor trying to keep the same action franchise going after half a century.

It seemed wrong that a man in his early forties should have to start worrying about getting older, but in a business where everyone was looking for the next 'new' face, it was a stress that was, sadly, well placed. Alex had so far shunned the surgeon's knife, and even the Botox needle, but knew that unless he switched gears and found a route away from his current screen idol persona, he would be destined to fall into the nip and tuck club before much longer.

He was resolute to not let that happen and was determined to make certain that *Hell After Dark* would be the vehicle that would shunt his acting career in an entirely different direction. Actors who have the chops to play anything and anyone are ultimately the survivors.

He planned to be one of them.

The black SUV pulled up in front of the old brick and white-picket-fenced patio of the famed restaurant. A uniformed valet opened the passenger door as a small herd of paparazzi appeared out of thin air and began jockeying for the best photo angle.

Alex had given up trying to hide from them. It was pointless and ultimately led to the vultures going to more devious lengths to get their candid shots. He'd learned that it was far easier to just give them a smile and a wave than have them try to find an ingress onto his property in the Hollywood Hills.

The moment Alex stepped out of the SUV, he heard the artificial sounds of their digital camera shutters. Some paps called for him to look their way, others even tried shouting pose suggestions. He ignored the requests as he gave them all a warm smile and a wave.

A woman screamed from up on the terrace as Alex saw diners diving to the ground. He then heard the sound of a car backfiring somewhere to his right. People began screaming. At first, he had no idea what was going on or why everyone seemed so upset, but as his left arm went numb and blood began saturating his white linen jacket, he realised that he was the reason for the ruckus.

He had no memory of the paramedics arriving only moments later. The fact that the restaurant was less than thirty seconds from Cedar Sinai hospital was a stroke of luck. He was in the emergency room within five minutes of the attack and was in surgery soon after that.

Nobody at the restaurant or on the sidewalk had seen the shooter's face. A few people had noticed someone in a grey hoodie jump up onto the terrace. A few even saw the gun, but once Alex had been shot, no one seemed to recall where the gunman (if it was a man) had gone. A 9mm Glock was recovered in one of the restaurant planters and the hoodie was found draped over one of the chairs closest to the pretty white fence.

It wasn't until the terrace had been cleared and the crime scene was being scrutinised that an envelope was found.

It was addressed to Alex Cole.

The lead detective eased open the unsealed flap and gently slipped the note free of the envelope. Holding it by one corner in her gloved hand, she was able to read the block letters.

THIS TIME IT WAS A WARNING
NEXT TIME YOU DIE.

3

CHAPTER

Vultures being what they are, the paparazzi had sensed that something was about to happen the moment the woman screamed and had changed their camera settings from still mode to video. Fourteen high-end cameras captured Alex being shot. Before the police had even arrived, they had all uploaded their footage to their own individual cloud storage apps as well as forwarding a GIF of the first few seconds of the footage to all the major celebrity photo sites so that electronic negotiations for the licensing rights could begin.

Within an hour of the shooting, various versions of the event were trending across the globe. The world was horrified. By the time the local news vans pulled up at the police cordons on Robertson Avenue, they were already too late. The digital world doesn't wait for broadcast breaking news anymore. The videos of Alex's shooting were viewed by over a billion people before he even came out of surgery.

Alex was extremely lucky. The bullet had passed through nothing but fatty tissue. Other than the entry and exit scars on his upper arm, he would be as good as new in plenty of time to start shooting his next movie.

Within two days, he was released to recuperate at home. The studio arranged for a live-in nurse for the first few days and a daily visit from his own doctor. In a rare display of restraint, other than a brief visit from Martha Hess, the studio suits gave Alex a couple of days of respite before descending on the house to ensure that their billion-dollar baby was really going to be able to carry on as before.

Codi had practically moved in and taken on the job of visitor coordinator for his friend. Everybody wanted to stop by and wish him well. Alex was doing well but didn't have the energy or the willingness to be around too many people at the same time. Being shot was far more complicated than he'd ever imagined. It wasn't just his body that needed to heal; it was his mind that had suffered the most. Codi understood that and did his best to turn Alex's home into a quiet refuge while he recovered. Alex couldn't help but smile as one of the world's most famous directors flitted around the ultra-modern hillside house, doting on Alex as if he was a compete invalid.

Then again, to some degree he was. Despite the dulling effect of the pain meds, Alex was a nervous wreck. Any noise in the house caused him to jump. Even the landline phone ringing was enough to trigger a near panic attack. Then there was the constant question that kept creeping into his head. 'Who wanted to shoot me and why?' He started unconsciously weighing up the potential 'real' intent of every person who asked to come by and wish him well. There was no doubt in his mind that he was becoming paranoid.

When Eva Morales, the lead detective on the case, came by to talk to him, Alex had been horrified to hear the amount of planning that the shooter must have gone through to get close enough to shoot him. That included his almost supernatural ability to be able to completely vanish once the shot was fired. It was also the first time that he'd learned about the note.

Other than Codi, the only visitors who had carte blanche to come and go were Alex's girlfriend, Linda Holt, and Diana Trent, Alex's manager for over fifteen years. Diana was short, petite and tomboyish. Her bob haircut and her wardrobe, which seemed to consist of nothing but jeans and white T-shirts, gave those meeting her for the first time the misguided belief that she was a lightweight. By their second meeting, if there was one, they knew better. Alex and Diana had grown up together in Arizona, and, after his first manager was poached by one of the top talent agencies, she was the only person he felt he could trust enough to take over the role.

The other constants in the house were Maria and Antonio Gonzales. Maria was not only the live-in cook and housekeeper but also managed Alex's two homes. Her husband Toni acted as driver, handyman and, at times, personal confidant. They had been with Alex for over ten years and had become such a big part of his life that he added an extension to the Hollywood Hills house, creating a cosy two-bedroom apartment with its own entrance and private backyard so they could live on the property. Not wishing to become separated from their friends and neighbourhood, they agreed to live at Alex's house but retained their small apartment in North Hollywood so they could regularly 'weekend' in the valley.

Though Toni was a third-generation Los Angelino, Maria's family history in California was far shorter.

Maria, her father and her mother had been shopping at the open-air Hermosillo Mercado in Northern Mexico. As her mother selected some fresh fruit to accompany their lunch, Maria, then only seven years old, heard firecrackers going off somewhere up ahead.

She thought she heard people screaming with joy at the festivities.

The sound got closer. Maria's father pushed his wife and daughter under a vegetable stand just as another volley of fireworks went off. Maria wasn't remotely scared. Her father often played hide and seek with her at their small casa on the outskirts of town.

More people screamed but this time Maria realised that they no longer sounded like screams of delight. These were the screams of people who were scared. As they lay quietly under the table, Maria heard new sounds. Some of the shoppers were crying.

When her mother finally felt that it was safe to emerge from their hiding place, Maria saw people lying amidst the fruit stalls. Her mother tried to shield her from seeing the bodies, but Maria was fascinated and wriggled loose. She stood above an older man who seemed to have a red stain on his shirt. He wasn't moving and his eyes seemed fixed as he stared up at the sky.

Maria then heard her mother cry out behind her. She turned and saw that her mother was looking down between two rows of produce. All Maria could see were the legs of someone who seemed to have collapsed onto one of the vendor stalls. Her mother saw Maria approaching and turned her the other way.

It was too late. Maria had recognised her father's shoes on the prone, unmoving body.

Her mother later learned that her husband had simply been standing in the wrong place at the wrong time. A rival cartel had gunned down three family members of a suspected informer during the family's weekly visit to the market. Maria's father had been hit by a stray bullet meant for someone else.

Sadly, even when shot in error, it didn't make the bullet any less lethal.

After a hastily arranged funeral, Maria's mother had sat her down and explained that they were leaving Hermosillo for good as the city had become too dangerous. They'd always known that, but had, like so many others, assumed that if they were not involved with the drug trade, they were somehow immune from the violence.

They were wrong.

Maria's mother had a sister who had moved to California almost a decade earlier and had begged that they leave Mexico so they could join her in the much safer city of Los Angeles. Many years earlier, her sister had married an American and together they had opened a Mexican restaurant only a few hundred yards from the MGM studios in Culver City. The business had boomed and the restaurant had expanded twice.

Her mother had helped Maria to pack. The two were waiting for the car that was to drive them to the Hermosillo Airport, from where they would fly to Phoenix, then on to LAX. Her sister's husband had some connection to someone in the Los Angeles mayor's office and had managed to arrange an emergency visa for the two of them.

As the car pulled up in front of their house, Maria looked through their net curtains expecting to see their old neighbour at the wheel as he had volunteered to drive them across town. Instead, two young men dressed in dark clothes got out of a newer model American car and approached the house.

Maria saw her mother's face darken as if a shadow had passed across it. She told her daughter to wait inside as she stepped out to speak to the men. Maria tried to hear what they were saying but couldn't. She could see, however, that her mother didn't seem to be doing any of the talking. Only the one man with a dark complexion and a scar on his neck spoke. She saw her mother cry but then nod.

She stepped back into the house and tried to sound as cheerful as possible though Maria could tell that she didn't feel cheerful at all. She explained to Maria that the nice men were going to drive them to the airport as their old neighbour had taken ill and couldn't leave his house.

They piled their belongings into the car and were driven across the city to General Ignacio L. Pesqueira International Airport. When they got there, the driver stopped at the curb and Maria and her mother gathered their cases from the trunk. The second man, the one with the scar, walked with them as they entered the terminal building. He stood off to one side as they checked in then accompanied them as they made their way to the departure gate.

Maria's mother kept trying to point out exciting and new sights to her daughter so as to lessen her pre-flight nerves. When they reached the gate, Maria watched as the man with the scar approached the airline check-in desk. He showed the two airline personnel what looked to be his identification, then turned and pointed directly at Maria.

Nothing more was said as the three sat in the departure lounge waiting for their flight to be called. Maria started to believe that the man with the scar was coming with them to California for some reason, though she couldn't understand why he would want to do that.

Just as the flight was being called, they were approached by one of the airline staff that the scar man had spoken to.

"Which one of you is Maria Chicquada?" the woman asked.

"I am," Maria replied.

"We board children first, so you need to come with me now."

Maria looked at her mother in horror. She didn't want to be separated for even a second.

"It's okay, my love. They always put children on first. It's safer that way."

Though she'd tried to sound as if everything was normal and happy, Maria could see the sadness in her mother's eyes.

"But Mama?"

"No, mi hija," she said stoically. "You get on the plane and get the seats ready. I'll be right there in a minute."

Maria was about to argue but then saw something in her mother's eyes that made her understand that she had to do this. The airline employee took Maria's hand and gently led her towards the waiting plane.

Maria turned just before starting down the jetway and saw her mother wave at her. She also saw the tears that were flowing down her face.

It was the last time she would ever see her mother.

As the 737 doorway was closed, Maria's mother turned to the man in black.

"You swear to me that she will never be hurt?" she pleaded.

"We don't kill young children."

"But you do kill their mothers," she said with resignation.

"Even though your husband's death was an accident, we can't leave any relatives alive to plot his revenge, can we?"

She slowly shook her head.

"You did very well today," he said. "You saved the life of your child."

"Thank you," she said with final resignation as the two walked out of the airport building.

When Maria arrived in Los Angeles, her aunt Selina was waiting at the arrival gate. She had expected to see Maria hand in hand with her sister. Instead, she was greeted with the sight of her niece, clearly overcome with emotion, being led through immigration by a flight attendant.

There was no sign of her sister.

And thus began Maria's auspicious start to life in Los Angeles.

Three days after the attack on Alex, Diana asked for him and Codi to meet with her to discuss security issues. They sat outside, next to the home's terrifying infinity pool. The borderless deep end gave the impression that the water flowed over the edge and down onto the canyon hundreds of feet below.

"I want to discuss increasing your security until the police find the person responsible," Diana began. "I would also like to cancel all of your upcoming public appearances as well."

"I will consider beefing up the security, but you know I can't cancel any of the events," Alex replied.

"The fans would understand," Diana insisted.

"My fans made me into a star and have kept me on top," Alex responded. "They look at me as a role model. How do you think they would feel if I blew them off just so I could hide up here in the hills in order to stay safe?"

"They'd think that you were being careful after someone tried to kill you," Diana said bluntly.

"I disagree. They've seen me get shot so many times and fight my way back that they expect this time to be no different."

"Those other times were in your films," Diana stressed. "This time was for real. Real gun, real bullet, real blood. They know the difference."

"Do they?" Alex asked. "Are you telling me that when fans think of Sylvester Stallone or Duane Johnson, they don't see them being able to take a bullet and get right back up to kick some ass? Of course, they do. That's what we've been selling all these years. That's why action stars have to keep up the tough guy act even when off-camera."

Diana was about to say something when Codi gently took her arm.

"He's right. It's crazy, but that's how it is," Codi explained. "Alex isn't saying that they really believe that he is the character he portrays, just that they only know him as an unstoppable tough guy. The better we are at making the acting and the effects seem real, the more the fans are going to buy the whole premise. I get what you are saying about Alex not putting himself out there while some shooter is stalking him, but simply cancelling the events will look like weakness on his part."

"But Alex *is* weak," Diana argued. "We all are. We can't actually jump out of a third-floor window then get up and chase the bad guy on foot. We can't be shot then fight off a dozen ninjas. What's on the screen is fantasy. What happened to you, Alex, is reality."

"Be that as it may, I'm not going to let my fans down, so you'll just have to ensure that I'm kept safe."

"Would you consider staying separated from the people at these events?" Diana suggested. "You could stay in the car and just wave to them."

"What, like a shady politician hiding behind tinted, bulletproof glass? Yeah, that's a great optic," Alex said, shaking his head. "I know you'll work something out."

"Have you heard anything else from the police?" Codi asked.

"Not a thing. The guy's a ghost," Alex advised.

"When's your next public event?" Codi asked.

"He's got a charity table reading with the rest of the original cast of *Deadly Recourse* at the Dolby Theater. It's being streamed on HMC but there's a live audience as well. It's next Thursday."

"It'll be fine," Alex insisted. "The Dolby hosts the Oscars. There isn't a safer venue anywhere."

Codi saw the look of concern on Diana's face.

"Keep him safe," Codi sighed.

4

CHAPTER

As the event wasn't to include a red-carpet arrival, the cast was able to take advantage of the Dolby Theater's underground security entrance. Toni drove Alex's Range Rover down a concrete ramp until they reached a gatehouse positioned just outside of a sliding steel-mesh garage door. The guard recognised Alex immediately but still followed protocol and asked to see both of their IDs.

The guard gave Toni directions as the metal door slid open on well-lubricated runners. Toni usually joined Alex on the set or in the green room for such events, but on this occasion, he was to stay with the vehicle to prevent any tampering or attempts at carjacking.

A line of wide-eyed production volunteers, all hoping to one day get their big Hollywood break, waited until their pre-assigned celebrity arrived. A young black woman in a severe business suit broke away from the pack and met Alex as he alighted from the SUV. She escorted him through the bowels of the building to a nondescript single-door elevator. The woman followed her training and didn't say a word. She was only to speak if spoken to.

"So, who are you and where are you from?" Alex asked.

"I'm Shana, and I'm from right here in Los Angeles, sir."

"Drop the sir…please," Alex smiled. "Where do you work, Shana from right here in Los Angeles?"

"I'm an undergrad at USC studying for my BA in Film Arts."

The elevator door opened and Shana led him to the backstage green room.

"This is as far as I go," Shana stated.

"Give it time. You'll get there," Alex smiled at her as he stepped into the room. He was immediately met with applause and warm greetings from the other members of the film cast. When they had shot the initial film of the *Deadly Recourse* series, none of them had expected there to be four sequels in what had become one of the most popular film franchises of its time.

After about half an hour of pleasantries, the eight stars were escorted onto the stage and took their pre-assigned seats at a long, linen-draped table. All eight faced the closed curtain beyond which was the packed auditorium filled with devoted fans. A single long-neck conference microphone sat before each participant.

After confirming that all eight were ready, the stage manager gave the signal for the curtain to be opened.

Ninety-eight minutes later, Alex read the last few lines of the script.

"Sure, I could just change everything about who I am and tell you that I love you, but it would be a hell of a lot easier if you could just shut up for a change and start having some fun."

The audience went nuts. The standing ovation lasted a full ten minutes. The streaming cameras cut off after the first two. As was the tradition at these public table reads, a select group, culled from the audience, was invited to stay behind for a Q and A session with the stars.

The questions were good, and the cast enjoyed the exchange. Just as the final question was answered, a young man at the front stood up and told them that he had an original prop from the film and wondered if they would autograph it for him. They agreed and he was led to the stairs at the side of the stage. As he walked towards the table, he reached into his jacket and pulled out a dark grey Uzi submachine gun.

Alex could see that the young man was smiling as he pointed it directly at him.

Three things happened in rapid succession:

Alex was tackled off his chair by security personnel and held concealed under the table.

Eight different male voices yelled "freeze" as security officers wielding H & K machine pistols appeared out of the shadows from the side of the stage.

The young fan pissed himself and started to cry.

He also dropped the prop gun onto the stage floor where the cheap plastic barrel snapped in two.

It took the cast and the event organisers over half an hour to calm the poor teen. He had never for a second considered the possible ramifications of pointing a gun, fake or not, at some of the biggest stars in Hollywood. The one thing that staff omitted from the post-trauma pep talk was that he was extraordinarily lucky not to have been shot dead himself.

The kid was finally driven home in an Uber limo with a swag bag full of memorabilia that the Dolby staff found in the back storage area. It was an attempt to make up for the rough treatment he'd received. The cast was more than happy to sign everything despite knowing full well that most of it would end up on eBay as soon as the guy's nerves healed a little.

What the cast was not told was that when the young man had been questioned in one of the empty dressing rooms, he explained that the prop gun wasn't even his. He'd been approached as he waited in line outside the venue by a guy who gave him the toy gun and told him what to do to guarantee that Alex would autograph it for him.

He couldn't describe the person as he had been wearing a hoodie and kept to the shadows.

The moment the poor fan had been dragged off stage, Alex was helped to his feet and quietly escorted back to the basement where Toni was waiting by the SUV with the passenger door open. Two members of the security detail that the theatre had hired for the event stood by until he was safely ensconced in the Range Rover and had been driven off the property.

Once again, phone footage of the incident was uploaded within minutes of the event. Alex's intent on making certain he continued to look heroic to his adoring fans was not helped by the viral video. The footage of him looking shocked only seconds before being tackled to the ground by security was not in line with his optic strategy in any way. His terrified expression became a trending meme within the first hour. GIFs of his shocked face edited onto clips cut from his most iconic movies followed soon after.

Alex was furious.

Social media was making him look comedically weak.

Days later, while Diana Trent was still trying to put out one PR fire after another, various associates and friends forwarded her a viral TikTok clip of the Dolby Theater debacle. On the video, instead of the eight cast members seated at a table, the clip creator had portrayed Alex wedged into a baby's highchair in the middle of the Dolby stage, reciting lines from *Deadly Recourse*.

Seeing a viral video satirising Alex Cole was not in the least bit unusual. There were millions of impressions and re-imagined images on the internet, some funny, some not.

This one was different. The man portraying Alex looked very like him. Scarily so. The hair was wrong, and the body language was off but other than that, it could have been him. He even nailed the voice. Diana asked her assistant to look at the video and he was convinced that it was the real Alex Cole.

Diana watched the clip over and over again for almost an hour.

She started to smile as the nucleus of an idea began to form in her mind.

5

CHAPTER

Alex, Diana, Martha, Codi and Herb Cohen, Alex's agent who had only just returned from a two-week trip to Australia, sat in the den/screening room in Alex's West Hollywood home in anticipation of Diana starting her presentation. Diana had invited them to see a short video. All she had said was that she had a fantastic idea on how to ensure Alex's safety until such time as the police had captured the man who had shot him. The den door opened, and Maria stepped aside to let Larry Fritt join the others.

He was a big man in his early sixties. Larry had retired after completing his 20 with the LAPD. He'd risen through the ranks to become a detective with the Hollywood Robbery-Homicide Division then had hit the political glass ceiling. His refusal to run his investigations according to the whims of the PR suits or the mayor's office stopped his having any further upward momentum. He ended up finishing his time with the RHD then starting his own small boutique security company catering to the special high-end needs of the major film studios. After greeting everyone, Larry took the last empty seat at the back of the room.

Diana mirrored the 120-inch curved-screen tv to her iPhone then darkened the room and pressed play. A montage of TikTok and Instagram videos showed the man from the highchair video. His one claim to fame seemed to be that he could impersonate Alex Cole. He mainly mimicked scenes from Alex's movies but occasionally had him in comic situations.

She showed one of him in a bubble bath reciting lines from *Angel Without a Heart,* and another where he was hanging upside down with his legs swung over a tree branch, satirising the famous final scene from Alex's hit, *Black Heart Pass.*

The strangest one of all was of the man competing in a local small-town talent competition. He walked onto the stage as himself. He was a little awkward and clearly very nervous. He introduced himself to the small crowd then announced that he was going to do a quick impression for them. the man turned away from the microphone, brushed his hair back with his fingers, then turned back around.

"You keep thinking that I don't feel anything when I have to put one of those assholes down. Well, you're wrong. It makes me feel… great."

His impression of Alex in *Hard Right on Third* was uncanny. In a split second, he became Alex Cole. It wasn't just a Jim Carrey type impression where he was able to contort his features into a decent caricature of the target. No. This guy actually looked almost exactly like Alex Cole even before the mimicry began.

Diana froze the video on a close shot of the man giving his best Alex Cole one-sided sneer that had become one of his most iconic cinematic facial expressions.

There was complete silence in the small room.

Codi was the first one to speak.

"Wow," he shook his head. "Looks like you have some serious competition, my friend."

He reached forward and patted Alex on the back.

"So, who is he?" Alex asked.

"His real name is Aaron Peterson," Larry Fritt replied. "He's an assistant manager of a chain hotel in Naples, Florida. He gave up on going to college when his folks died in a house fire when he was fifteen. He doesn't have a police record. There's no family that we could find. He's third-generation American from an eastern European background and he seems to be in perfect health except for an allergy to penicillin."

"My thinking is that we bring the guy out here," Diana suggested, "and give him some training from the one person who knows Alex the best…"

She turned to face Alex then grinned.

"Oh Christ," Alex sighed.

"…then have Mr Peterson fill in for Alex at any public events until the situation changes. While he's in town, he'll stay in your guest house and remain isolated from the outside world until such times as we need him to be you."

"Why would anyone want to do that?" Alex asked.

"Money," Larry answered. "The guy isn't exactly starving but he's not living life large, either. You offer him some decent green with a nice completion bonus if he performs well, and I would bet that he'll be on the next plane out of Fort Meyers."

"I don't know," Alex looked back at Codi. "What do you think?"

"I think it's an interesting option. Let's face facts—the last two times you've been out in public didn't exactly go that well. You got shot the first time and thought you were going to get shot the second time. Personally, I don't think you should risk a third one, do you?"

"What happens if we get found out?" Alex asked.

"As long as only one of you is visible out of the house at any one time, I see the risk as minimal," Larry advised. "If this Aaron guy follows the script and doesn't go rogue, we'll be fine."

"That didn't answer my question," Alex insisted. "What if we get busted. All it would take is a picture of me at home, or in the pool at the same time as I'm on stage at Comic-Con and I'm done. I'd be crucified. I'd end up being the Milli Vanilli of Hollywood."

From the expressions in the room, only about half the attendees got the vintage reference to the male singing duo who got busted for lip-syncing at live concerts and hardly ever worked again.

"How many live appearances do you have in the next month?" Larry asked.

"Eleven public events," Herb advised. "But then there are some private dinners and meetings as well."

"I don't care about the meetings and dinners," Alex said. "We can move the meetings here if we have to and postpone the dinners. I'm only interested in the public-facing stuff."

"It's the twentieth anniversary of *Young Stallion*," Diana reminded him. "You're booked on every talk show in town as well as the whole late-night circuit."

"Shit. Well, there's no way some mimic from Florida can stand in for me on the Tonight Show, is there?"

"The late-night shows are all in four weeks; let's worry about the local gigs first," Diana suggested. "Why don't we get the guy out here and see just how good he really is? As far as the anniversary interviews, all we have to do is prep him for what will almost certainly be the same bunch of questions from all of the hosts."

"I can be in Naples first thing tomorrow," Larry offered.

Alex paced the front of the screening room trying to decide what to do. He stopped in front of the paused image on the curved screen. He studied the other man's face.

"The hair's wrong," he stated.

"We know," Diana replied. "That'll only take a few hours to fix."

"The eyes are the wrong colour."

"Contacts," Codi replied.

"His voice is a little higher than mine," Alex added.

"So, we train him to speak lower," Diana countered. "Look, the guy's your doppelganger. All that's needed is some fine-tuning."

"What if he turns out to be a complete nut job? What then?"

"I take him back to Florida; he doesn't get his back-end payment and we deny ever having met the guy," Larry replied. "He'll have signed a non-disclosure agreement, so he wouldn't be stupid enough to try and go public. Besides, from everything that I saw in the initial report from SFI, Peterson is a nobody. He's got no record, no debts, no questionable affiliation, which, considering where he lives, is kinda refreshing. I just don't see the guy doing anything but following instructions, then, in a few weeks, he'll go back home with a hell of a lot of money in his pocket."

"I hope you're right, Larry," Alex said with a sigh as he took one last look at the screen.

"I give up. Go get him."

Larry took the United red-eye from LAX to Miami then rented a midsized sedan from Enterprise. The drive across the Everglades on Highway 41 took just over two hours. It was still dark out and the sheer blackness of the swamplands on either side of the road gave him the chills. By the glow of one of the infrequent streetlights, he saw what had to have been a ten-foot gator slide off the raised roadside verge and glide into a deep drainage channel that paralleled the highway.

Larry stopped at a greasy spoon just south of Naples and had breakfast. After a quick wash in the restaurant's men's room, he followed the car's GPS to 197 N Tamiami Trail. He pulled into the forecourt of the Rancho Suites Motel and turned off the engine. It was too early for the day shift to have arrived, but, according to Larry's contacts, Aaron worked from midnight to eight in the morning.

He opened the car door and was assaulted by a blast of impossible heat. It had still been dark when he'd stopped for breakfast. Now that the sun was starting to crawl up the eastern sky, the temperature and humidity were already off the charts. He could feel his clothes starting to stick to his body after only walking a few feet to the motel entrance.

As he reached a darkly tinted door, it slid noiselessly aside. He could instantly feel refrigerated air clawing to get out. For a brief moment, his body had intense heat on one side and what felt like an arctic blast on the other.

The lobby was generic, comfortable in a bland sort of way and empty of guests. Larry could hear people attacking the complimentary breakfast buffet in an adjoining space. The reception desk filled one wall. Behind it was a mural depicting Naples beach at sunset. Larry got the feeling that the artist probably used the same theme, except of course for a few Naples-specific images, for every one of their three hundred locations.

Standing directly under the depiction of the city's historic pier was Aaron Peterson. He gave Larry a welcoming smile that sent a shiver down Larry's back. Diana's videos hadn't done him justice.

The man looked exactly like Alex Cole if Alex had ever worn cheap polyester, had a threadbare goatee and sported a mullet.

"Welcome to Rancho Suites," Aaron announced.

Larry was momentarily taken aback that the voice sounded nothing like Alex. It was eerie seeing the face of the star but hearing the voice of a nobody.

"Are you checking in?" Aaron asked.

"Actually, I'm here to see you, Mr Peterson."

Aaron raised his eyebrows but didn't seem remotely fazed by Larry's words. Clearly, he wasn't carrying the kind of guilt that would make a man rack his brain about what he could have done wrong to necessitate a personal caller at work.

"I can't image why," Aaron said with a smile.

"I'm here on behalf of Alex Cole," Larry stated.

"Nice one," Aaron laughed.

"I'm serious. Alex saw your impressions and wanted me to come out here and get to know a little more about you."

"Is this a legal thing? As far as I know, doing impressions online isn't against the law. I mean, I've never been paid to do them."

"Actually, that's why I'm here," Larry announced. "We might be interested in offering you a short-term assignment."

A sunburned and morbidly overweight couple emerged from the breakfast room with plates piled high with assorted pastries. They made for the reception desk and waited a few steps behind Larry.

"I'm the only one on duty at the desk until eight o'clock. Do you mind waiting until then?" Aaron said to Larry. "There's a guest lounge with a TV just down the hall."

"No problem," Larry replied. "Any chance of my grabbing a coffee?"

"Of course. Help yourself to the buffet as well if you like."

Larry glance at the overflowing plates behind him then glanced back at Aaron.

"If there's any left," he said in a stage whisper as he moved away from the reception desk.

Larry found a comfortable corner in the lounge and spent the time reading a *Harry Bosch* novel on his phone's Kindle app. The fictional character worked the same streets and divisions as he had during his time on the force. While the literary detective's cases were usually far more exciting and complex than Larry's had ever been, the author had nailed the process, the procedures and the political bullshit that Larry had gone through on a daily basis.

At eight sharp, Aaron stepped into the lounge.

"What can I do for you, Mister…?" Aaron asked.

"Fritt. Larry Fritt," he replied as he got to his feet.

They shook hands.

"Can we talk in here?" Larry asked.

"As good a place as any," Aaron replied.

He positioned a chair so he could face Larry.

"So, what does the great Alex Cole want from me?" Aaron asked.

Larry explained the situation in LA and the idea that Diana had put forward. When he'd finished, he sat back in his chair and looked to Aaron for some sort of reaction.

"Let's see if I've got this straight. You came all the way out here from the west coast to see if I wanted to fill in for Alex Cole at a bunch of public events just because someone is trying to kill him?"

"Basically, yes." Larry nodded.

"In doing so, wouldn't I, in effect, be putting myself in extreme danger? I saw the video of him being shot. It was nasty. I mean, if I do my job perfectly and succeed at being mistaken for Alex Cole, surely the stalker, or whatever he is, would most likely try to kill me, wouldn't he?"

"We would ensure that you would always be surrounded by heavy security whenever you were in public," Larry offered.

"If that was a sufficient deterrent, you wouldn't be here, isn't that correct?" Aaron countered.

"I can't say that there's no risk, but now that we are aware of the threat, I don't see how anyone could get to Alex… or to you, for that matter."

"What, like that poor kid at the Dolby Theater? The one who walked in with a machine gun under his jacket?"

"It wasn't a machine gun. It was a toy," Larry said emphatically.

"Potato, patato. It could just as easily have been the real deal," Aaron insisted.

"Look, there is obviously some risk. You know that and we know that. That's why we're willing to pay you very well for your time."

"Define very well?" Aaron asked bluntly.

"A thousand dollars a day and a ten-thousand-dollar bonus upon successful completion of the project."

"I'm the project?" Aaron smiled.

"For the want of a better term…yes," Larry replied.

"What if the guy is never caught?" Aaron asked. "Does this become a full-time gig?"

"No," Larry smiled. "First of all, the person will be caught. They always are. If, for some inexplicable reason, he isn't, we will have to make different arrangements."

"Like what?"

Larry gave him a cold smile.

"That will be for Alex's team to work out."

"So, how long would I be in LA?" Aaron asked.

"Until he begins shooting *Hell After Dark.* That starts in just over six weeks."

"You expect me to quit my job with Rancho Suites just for a six-week gig?"

"If you accept the position, Rancho Suites will receive an offer from Magnum Pictures to give the company free product placement in Alex's next film. There will be one specific caveat to the free publicity offer. They have to guarantee that you still have a job with them when this assignment is all over."

"What about expenses?" Aaron asked with a cheeky smile.

"You won't have any. You'll be living at Alex's house. Anything you need will be bought for you."

"Like a Ferrari?" he asked.

"Nobody needs a Ferrari," Larry replied.

Aaron stared down at his lap as he thought over what was being offered.

"You guys must really think my impressions of Alex are good."

"They are good," Larry stated.

"Then pay me what the hell I'm worth," Aaron shot back in a flawless Alex Cole delivery. "Fifteen hundred a day and twenty K on the backend."

"You're quite a negotiator for an assistant chain-motel manager," Larry observed.

Aaron stared at the other man with one eyebrow raised and his teeth clenched.

"It's not what I do that matters. It's who I am that makes the big difference." The line from Deadly Recourse II was delivered exactly as Alex had done twelve years earlier.

Larry felt the hair rise on the back of his neck.

6

CHAPTER

Larry followed Aaron to his small apartment on the east side of town so he could pack a few things to take with him to Los Angeles. Aaron left his car baking in the midmorning sun as Larry drove them back along HWY 41 to Miami. Instead of following the signs to the main domestic terminal, Larry followed the GPS route to the general aviation area.

A seven-seater Gulf Stream G-100 was waiting at the executive terminal. Larry arranged for the rental car to be picked up then escorted Aaron on board the luxurious aircraft.

He could see that Aaron seemed especially nervous as he settled himself into one of the cream-coloured leather seats.

"You alright?" he asked.

Aaron glanced out the Gulf Steam's square window to try and disguise his fear.

"Never been in a private jet?" Larry asked.

"Never been in any jet," Aaron replied.

"You'll be fine. You had more chance of dying driving to work this morning than of this plane going down."

"Why aren't we flying commercial?" Aaron asked. "This has to be costing a fortune."

"From now on, you are a ghost. Nobody is to see you unless you are standing in for Alex. As for the cost, this is one of the studio jets so it's not costing Alex anything."

"If we were gonna go private, why didn't we fly from Naples Airport?" Aaron asked. "It was a lot closer."

"People know you in Naples. It might have been difficult to explain what you were doing getting into a Gulf Stream."

"You must have been pretty sure that I was going to say yes to have a jet sitting waiting for us."

Larry smiled.

"It was on the east coast anyway. I texted my people when you were letting your co-workers know that you weren't going to be around for a while. They had the plane fly down from Orlando."

A uniformed pilot stepped out of the cockpit and smiled at the two passengers.

"If you two are ready, we'll get moving."

"Light her up," Larry replied.

The take-off was flawless. The mid-sized jet shot up to its cruising altitude in half the time it would have taken a commercial jet. Coffee, soft drinks and a selection of sandwiches were stowed in a forward service cabinet.

Two hours into the five-hour flight, Larry's phone chirped. He had a brief conversation then walked up to the cockpit and spoke to the pilots.

"Everything alright?" Aaron asked nervously when Larry returned to his seat.

"Everything's fine. We're not going to fly into LA. Alex and his people decided that it would be far more private and comfortable if you did your training at Villa Miranda."

Aaron gave the other man a puzzled look.

"That's Alex's second home. You get to stay in Montecito!"

"Big whoop," Aaron responded sullenly.

"Actually, it is a big whoop. Very few people get to visit the Montecito estate. It's very special to Alex."

"I was looking forward to seeing Los Angeles," Aaron said.

"You will, don't worry."

"Who's Miranda?" Aaron asked.

"I thought you were some sort of expert on Alex Cole."

"I never said I was. I just do a good impression of the guy. I'm actually not that big of a fan."

"Now you tell me," Larry replied sarcastically.

"Does it matter?"

"Hopefully not," Larry answered.

"So, who was she?"

"Miranda Adams was Alex's wife."

"Was?"

"Boy, you really don't know much about him, do you?" Larry commented.

Aaron shrugged.

"Miranda died of leukaemia four years ago," Larry explained. "They remodelled the Montecito house together and used to keep it for when they wanted to be by themselves and away from the rest of the world."

"I thought Alex was dating Linda Holt?"

"He is but that's only been for the past year and a half," Larry explained.

"You'd think a guy in his position, someone who could have any woman he wanted, would be playing the field instead of being such a boring monogamist. I mean, I would be screwing a different woman every night. Wouldn't you?" Aaron said shaking his head.

"Actually, I was married to the same woman for eighteen years until she died last year. As for Linda, she is the only person he's dated since Miranda's death."

"Wow. What is wrong with you guys?"

Larry forced a smile. Inside, a tiny alarm bell had gone off though he wasn't sure why. Did it really matter that the guy was shallow as hell and not that big a fan of Alex?

The plane touched down at Santa Barbara Municipal Airport at 12:30 pm. Toni was waiting at the private terminal, and, within fifteen minutes of their landing, they pulled up at a nondescript wrought iron gate surrounded by oleander hedging. A digital keypad sat nestled within a steel enclosure.

It wasn't until they had driven through the gate and crested the landscaped hill that Aaron got his first view of Villa Miranda. It was a two-storey, 5000 square foot Mediterranean-styled home surrounded by immaculate lawns and perfectly trimmed Cypress trees. The property was shielded by vegetation on three sides giving complete privacy from the hill behind and the neighbours on either side. The fourth one offered an unobstructed view of the bay and the Channel Islands beyond.

As Toni drove up to the front entrance, Aaron saw a group of people sitting out on a front patio watching his arrival. Alex Cole waved and got to his feet. A small woman, whom Larry advised was his manager, followed the star as he made his way to greet his guests. A third person that Aaron recognised as Linda Holt remained on the terrace. Even seated, he could see that her photos didn't do her justice. Her long auburn hair and naturally tanned skin looked almost airbrushed. She'd been an A-list actress when she had suddenly quit the business and begun painting. Her abstracts now hung in galleries across the globe.

The only sign that she'd even noticed the new arrivals was when she lowered her oversized sunglasses to have a quick peek at the man who was going to pretend that he was Alex Cole. Just as Aaron was about to offer his best crooked smile, she flipped the glasses back up and turned away.

"Welcome to Villa Miranda," Alex said as he shook Aaron's hand. "How was the flight?"

"It was his first," Larry offered.

"Then it must have been quite an experience," Alex said.

"I don't have anything to compare it to," Aaron answered as he closely studied the other man. He was surprised to find little facial flaws that he never knew existed - a small scar on his chin, an acne pock on his right cheek, even a few shaving nicks that Aaron hadn't expected to see on one of the most famous faces in the world.

"Aaron, I hope I may call you that…?" Alex began.

"Sure. It's my name."

"Aaron, this is Diana Trent. She's my manager and the person who brought you to my attention."

"It's nice to meet you, Aaron. Your online videos are fabulous."

"Well, aren't you a whole lot of dynamite in a small package," Aaron mimicked from one of Alex's films.

Diana continued to smile but had seen something in the man's eyes that gave her pause. Though he'd been smiling while saying the line, Aaron's eyes had been cold as if he was closely calculating her reaction to his impression.

"That's good," she said. "Very good. I can't wait to see what you look like without the beard and after hair and makeup have finished with you."

Aaron knew full well that she had fully intended for her words to knock a little of his cockiness away. She'd managed to let him know that without a lot of work, he was still a nobody. And she had done it while holding his hand and smiling like an angel.

He realised at that moment that he was going to have to keep his guard up with that one.

7

CHAPTER

Once inside the house, Aaron was introduced to Maria who didn't seem the least bit fazed about showing an exact replica of her employer to a guest suite at the back of the house. Aaron had no idea what to expect, but when she opened the double oak doors, he was stunned. The suite consisted of a split-level sitting room with adjoining bedroom and ensuite bathroom. The flooring was terracotta-tiled and the walls were rough plastered and painted a bright matte white. The furniture was dark wood and had a Spanish feel. A pair of white overstuffed couches sat on either side of a huge brick fireplace. Between them was what looked to be an antique church door that had been converted into a coffee table.

Aaron had never seen such luxury in all his life. He liked it. The moment Maria had left and closed the door, he flopped down on one of the couches and sighed as he sank into its decadent softness. He knew that the ultra-rich lived like this but had never been in a position to appreciate what that meant first-hand.

In one day, he'd gone from working at a low-end chain hotel to being flown in a private jet to a mansion hidden away in the hills above the Pacific Ocean. Even stranger still was that it was all because of his happening to look like some other guy.

Aaron spent much of the afternoon trying on a selection of clothes that Alex's people had bought for him. He'd been told to only keep the stuff he liked.

He liked them all.

It had never dawned on him that the clothes that rich people wore actually felt better. The fabric was softer and more comfortable. Even the underwear was different. He'd always been perfectly happy with the three-packs of Calvin Klein briefs he'd been buying his whole life from Ross or Marshall's, depending on which store was selling them for less.

At six, as arranged, Aaron emerged from his room and joined the others for a drink before dinner. He wore a pair of brand-new black linen trousers and a cream-coloured silk shirt that must have cost more than he normally earned in a week.

He followed the sound of voices and found Alex, Linda and Diana sitting in a wood-panelled room that overlooked the bay. Folding glass doors were open allowing the scent of jasmine and pine to perfume the air.

"Aaron," Alex greeted him warmly. "Come join us."

Aaron sat in a huge armchair that was so soft, his initial reaction was one of concern that he would keep sinking into the plush cushioning until his butt eventually reached the floor. Toni appeared almost magically and asked what he would like to drink.

At home, Aaron only drank beer. It wasn't so much that he liked the stuff, it was more the fact that he could buy a 30-pack of Bud-Lite on sale at Costco for under twenty bucks.

"What are you guys having?" he asked.

"Linda and I are drinking a Sauvignon Blanc that we found in Sonoma last year," Diana replied. "And Alex is having his usual gin and tonic. You don't have to follow our lead. You can have anything you want."

"If I'm going to fit in, I should probably have one of those gin and tonics like Alex is having."

Toni smiled and silently exited the room. Linda picked up a large white platter off the coffee table and held it out for Aaron. On it were toast wedges fanned out on one side of the dish and curls of smoked salmon, olive tapenade, and ultra-thin slices of beef carpaccio.

Nothing was familiar to him, but he followed instructions from Diana and prepared a small plate for himself. He desperately wanted to ask if that was all they were having for dinner as he was starving. He decided just to wait and see so as not to embarrass himself more than he had to.

He loved the salmon and the beef but as far as he was concerned, the tapenade tasted exactly like what it was… ground olives. He wasn't a fan of olives except on a pizza, but he at least gave it a try.

Toni reappeared and set a chunky crystal glass on the table in front of him. Aaron noticed that it was half full of clear liquid, ice and a thin slice of lemon. Toni started to pour tonic from an individual bottle and waited for Aaron to say when he should stop.

"I like them strong, so I usually put in about half the tonic," Alex suggested.

Aaron smiled up at Toni and nodded.

"To our new friend and house guest," Alex raised his glass in a toast.

"Thank you for bringing me here," Aaron toasted back. As he took his first sip of the drink, he could taste the subtle sour flavour of the juniper berries mixed with the dry sweetness of the tonic.

"Wow, these are good."

"The way Alex drinks them, they're also strong, so go easy," Diana suggested.

"So, what are your interests, Aaron?" Alex asked.

"I like boats, the movies, obviously, and television, I guess," he replied with a shrug.

"I have a boat here at the marina. Maybe I could take you out on her if you're interested," Alex offered.

"That would be really cool. Thank you," Aaron replied.

"I hate to be a killjoy, but is that a good idea when you and Aaron aren't supposed to be seen together?" Diana mentioned.

"Relax. We'll go down one night after dinner when it's dark and do a few circuits of the bay. No one will see a thing."

Aaron started peppering Alex with numerous fan-like questions about his movies and especially about some of his leading ladies.

"What's it like getting to make out with so many beautiful film stars?" Aaron asked.

"Actually, when we kiss on screen, there's nothing romantic or sexual about it. It's just another part of acting."

"Come on! Are you telling me that when you kissed Cindy Snow in Deadly Recourse III, you weren't feeling anything?"

"That's a great example," Alex nodded. "Cindy and I have been friends since the soap opera days. She's more like a sister to me. Every time we had to kiss in that movie, she would get the giggles. If you'd been there, you would have seen that there was nothing exciting about it at all. It worked on screen because of the lighting, the music and some decent acting."

"What a waste," Aaron said, sounding very disappointed.

"I take it you like Cindy Snow, huh?" Alex asked, amused.

"God, yeah."

"I'll tell you what, Aaron. If all this works out, how about my introducing her to you?"

"You'd do that?" he asked, stunned.

"Sure. She'll get a kick out of meeting you," Alex replied.

"Why wait until it's all over?" Diana asked. "We've been trying to work out the best way to test Aaron to see if he really can fool everyone. Why not try him out with Cindy when he's ready? If he can fool her, he can fool anybody. Plus, we know that she will keep the whole body-double thing a secret."

"Are you suggesting doing that without telling her what's going on?" Linda Holt asked. "That seems a little mean."

"I still owe her for the two hookers she sent up to my room in Thailand!" Alex advised.

"Excuse me?" Linda asked in a colder tone.

"It was a joke. They were male and they didn't even get through security," Alex explained. "I think passing Aaron off as me would make us even. When the time comes, are you ready for that sort of pressure, Aaron?"

"With Cindy Snow? Fuck, yeah!"

There was a moment of dead silence after the exclamation, then Alex howled with laughter. The others followed but Diana couldn't help but notice the look that had flashed across Aaron's features.

It made her think of Jack Nicholson's expression when he was being interviewed for the winter caretaker position in the movie *The Shining.* Aaron had looked innocently excited while at the same time just a little crazy. She decided that she was being overly paranoid about letting this guy get within the inner circle of Alex's life. Diana knew that Larry had done every background check possible, but something about Aaron worried her.

Her thoughts were interrupted as Toni gently announced that dinner was ready. The four walked to the back of the house and into a surprisingly intimate dining room. An oak table was set for four.

Aaron had no idea if it was to make him feel comfortable or not, but the dinner consisted of spaghetti Bolognese, a mixed green salad and hot garlic bread. The food was delicious and unostentatious. Alex told Aaron stories of funny on-set mishaps that he'd never heard before.

Aaron was enthralled.

After dinner, Alex asked if Aaron had seen the latest sequel to *Final Haunting*.

"No. How could I?" It's not out for another two weeks!" Aaron replied.

Alex gave him a knowing wink.

He led Aaron down a short hallway then opened a nondescript wooden door. Behind it was another door that looked to have been made from solid steel. Instead of a handle, there was an illuminated keypad as part of a control panel. Alex entered eight numbers and the door slid silently open.

Carpeted stairs led down to a screening room which seemed to also double as a man cave. It was decorated in dark shades of grey with twelve plush theatre seats arranged on a gently raked riser. There was a Ludwig drum kit against one wall next to a Marshall stack and a guitar rack filled with some serious axes. The ladies followed them down into the room and smiled at the expression on Aaron's face. He looked like a young boy on Christmas morning looking at all the presents under the tree.

"Looks like you enjoy making a lot of noise," Aaron said as he nodded towards the drums and amp.

"I'm afraid I do, but the room's completely soundproofed from the rest of the house. It's my little fortress of solitude."

"Nice," Aaron replied with a smile.

As soon as they were seated, Alex pressed a button on an armrest console.

"We're ready when you are, Toni."

8

CHAPTER

The following day, Aaron showered and shaved off his early-stage goatee. He felt a little sad at having to let it go, but he recognised that it could never be part of a serious Alex Cole impression; besides, he'd only been growing it for a few days.

Wrapped in the whitest and softest terry cloth robe he'd ever seen or felt, Aaron ate breakfast alone in his suite. Maria had checked with him the night before to find out his favourites. After tucking away two waffles, scrambled eggs and six rashers of extra crispy bacon, Aaron walked into the far wing of the house and located Alex's private office. He knocked timidly on the door.

"Come on in, Aaron," Alex replied.

Aaron stepped into the room and felt his knees go weak. The room was big. Two walls were filled with one-sheets from every movie that Alex had ever been in. Another had built-in under-lit shelving that held all his film and TV awards. Starting on the far left were the Emmy's he'd won for his role as Jake Fallen on the soap opera *Days and Nights*. The collection ended with his Oscar for best actor in *Hard Men Still Bleed*.

Dotted around the room were some of the best-known props from some of the most iconic movies ever made. The coolest by far was the life-size model of the creature from Ridley Scott's space horror, *Alien*.

"How'd you sleep?" Alex asked.

It took a moment for Aaron to answer. He was so distracted by the contents of the room that he could hardly think straight.

"Fine, I guess. That bed was like sleeping on a cloud."

"Glad you liked it," Alex smiled. "Well, if you're ready, it's time that you learned everything about me."

The two men spent the next three days locked away in Alex's office. Lunch was eaten in the room as the lessons continued. Even when they broke for the day, Alex would pepper him during cocktail hour and over dinner with questions about what he'd learned so far that day.

Aaron had expected that learning everything about the star would be fun. It was anything but. He hadn't realised the depth of knowledge he was expected to memorise. It wasn't just about big things like his hometown or close friends. It was minutia like knowing his favourite fruit, what toothpaste he used, his top twenty favourite foods. The worst part by far was what Alex called his face recognition data dump.

When Aaron first sat down in Alex's study, he'd been given an iPad mini that had all the knowledge he was meant to learn and remember. Someone had even programmed a digital Q & A quiz that covered every single aspect that Aaron had been taught.

The facial recognition part of the data dump was the hardest part for Aaron to learn. There was a photo library of every single person that Alex knew. Under each picture were the individual's name, job, connection to Alex, years known and any other extraneous information that someone had deemed necessary.

There were hundreds of people from dozens of countries. By the end of the third day, Aaron was expected to score 100% on the iPad quiz, including the facial recognition module. No matter how hard he tried, he kept messing up the picture section. Alex made a deal with him. The day he aced the quiz, he'd take Aaron out on the boat as a reward for his hard work.

Aaron was up for the challenge. He needed to get out of the house. He was starting to get cabin fever being cooped up in there day after day. Even the most palatial home lost some of its lustre when you were imprisoned within it. Aaron studied the photo module every moment he wasn't in class, eating or sleeping.

At the end of the first week's instruction, a black SUV with tinted windows pulled up in front of the house. Aaron was intrigued as he watched two women, along with Toni and Maria, unload a slew of reinforced aluminium travel cases from the back of the SUV and bring them into the house.

Alex appeared from his study and greeted the two guests with hugs and kisses.

"Aaron," he called. "Come and meet Sheila and Evelyn. We thought we'd surprise you today with your first makeover."

Aaron gave Alex a concerned look.

"Sheila here has been my makeup artist for twenty years and Evelyn's been stuck doing my hair for over fifteen."

"I understand the hair, but I don't want to wear any makeup," Aaron stated.

"I know that you already think you look exactly like me but under camera lights and hi-res cameras, there are some areas that are going to need a little work."

Aaron approached Alex and whispered, "I thought nobody was to know about this?"

"These two lovely ladies know me better than I do. When you're stuck on location in the middle of nowhere, you learn to know who you can trust. These two have seen me at my worst and best."

Sheila held out her hand and tipped it back and forth. "Best?"

Alex laughed.

"They basically have to live in my trailer and stay within spitting distance for the entire shoot. I trust them with my life."

Aaron still looked dubious.

"Are you saying that Sheila's going to have to make me up every single time I step outside?"

"God, I hope not," Sheila jumped in.

As she approached him, Aaron could see that she was older than he'd first thought. Also, by the way she walked, she looked much tougher and gave the impression that she could take care of herself in just about any situation. Her super-short dark hair, and strong, almost manly features, made him wonder if she was into women more than men. That was one thing he just couldn't understand. If a girl got the chance for a nice hard cock, why the hell would she opt for nothing but bush?

Aaron flinched as Sheila reached out to touch his face. For a split second, he wondered if she'd somehow read his thoughts and was about to slap him. Instead, she took hold of his chin and tilted his head back. She then turned it slightly to the left and then to the right.

"You're right, Alex," she said. "His chin is a little weaker than yours. I think we can fix that with a little shading here and here."

She ran her index finger along the underside of his face. Sheila then stepped very close to him and stared into his eyes. Aaron felt exceedingly uncomfortable. She was totally invading his space. He couldn't even remember a time when a woman had been that close without it getting interesting.

"Obviously, the eye colour is wrong but that'll just need tinted contacts. The bigger issue is that his eyes are set further back than yours. I didn't notice it on the videos but on a TV soundstage, the lights will pick it up."

"What can you do?" Alex asked.

"I think I can lighten under the brow. That should take away some of the shadowing. Evelyn, what do you think?"

Evelyn approached Aaron and looked at him closely. Aaron wanted to back away. Having a black woman stand so close to him just felt wrong. He tried not to show his displeasure but didn't do that good a job of it.

"I think you're right. I also think he's going to have to learn not to show such disdain when someone of colour gets too close to him."

Sheila stood back and stared hard at Aaron as she shook her head.

"You're going to have to be completely clean-shaven every time you're standing in for Alex. Your natural beard is much darker than his. Alex doesn't get a five o'clock. You do."

"I'll shave every morning," Aaron replied defensively.

"That won't be enough," Sheila continued. "Your beard will show on camera as early as mid-afternoon. You could always apply a heavy pancake, but I think you'd prefer to just shave."

"Me, apply make-up?" Aaron stammered.

"Yup. My job today is to find the most basic make-up regime that you will be able to do yourself. I'm hoping that what I have in mind will take you less than half an hour once you get the hang of it."

"How am I supposed to get the hang of putting on make-up? Only girly boys put on make-up."

"I wear makeup every time I go on camera. Do you think I'm a girly boy, Aaron?" Alex said as he shook his head.

"God, no, but…"

"But, what?" Alex pushed.

"I don't want people to think I'm some kind of a faggot," Aaron stated.

"Wow," Sheila exclaimed.

"You're going to need to either change your outlook on other people's sexual orientation or if you can't do that, find a way to bury it," Alex stated. "People are entitled to be whoever they want to be, so, whatever prejudices you might have—you need to can them right this second. Do you understand me?"

Alex's tone had lost its friendly edge. He disliked intolerance and never shied away from confronting a hater.

"I'm sorry, Alex," Aaron said. "I didn't realise you like that sort of stuff."

Alex's colour darkened and Sheila could see the storm that was coming any second. She had worked with Alex for long enough to know when he was gonna blow. It was a rare occurrence but was always memorable when it did happen.

"Why don't you leave the poor misguided little man to us?" Sheila suggested. "We can set him straight while we try to make him look as good as you."

Alex nodded but it was obvious that he was steamed over the revelation that Aaron seemed to be stuck in some outdated bigot world. He could suddenly imagine seeing Aaron standing screaming and waving at one of those mega political rallies they used to have in the southern states.

Sheila took Aaron roughly by the arm and led him down the hallway. "The three of us are gonna have a ball, aren't we, Evelyn?"

"Oh yeah. It's not often that we get to do a makeover on the inside as well as the outside."

9

CHAPTER

Three hours later, the two women sat Alex in the living room, then, with theatrical aplomb, drew back a heavy window curtain revealing the new Aaron.

Alex had asked for Maria and Toni to be with him for the transformation reveal. Aaron gave the three his best crooked-mouth smile. Toni gave a brief hand clap. Maria looked as if she'd seen a ghost. She stepped closer and studied his features.

"This is creepy," she stated in her heavily accented voice. "I only like seeing one of you in this house."

With that, she strode back towards the kitchen.

"What do you think?" Sheila asked, smiling towards Alex.

"You both did great. Did he give you any trouble?"

"Not at all. Evelyn and I had a nice little chat about how to behave from now on. I think he understood."

"Did you?" Alex asked Aaron.

Aaron nodded and shot Evelyn and Sheila a concerned glance. He had never been talked to the way those two broads had laid into him. It wasn't as if they could really expect him to change who he was but he sure as hell now knew to keep certain thoughts to himself.

"Good," Alex stated. "Now let's see what they've done to you."

Alex approached him and stared openly from a couple of different angles.

"Do one of your impressions of me," he asked.

Aaron stood a little taller. His shoulders rounded slightly as he tucked his hands into his trouser pockets.

"Doesn't look to me like these guys had much of a chance. Shame. I woulda paid to have had a little quiet time with them. I'll say one thing. Whoever chopped up these boys seemed to enjoy their work. Hell, it's gonna take the coroner half a day just to match the pieces back together," Aaron quoted.

Alex looked to Toni then to Evelyn and Sheila. All three of them were grinning.

"Wow. If I didn't know better, I'd swear I was looking at me," Alex announced. "How much of what you did is repeatable by Aaron when you're not around?"

"All of it," Sheila said proudly. "The contacts are colour only, no prescription, so he'll have to practice getting them in and out, but that'll become second nature. The makeup was harder, but we found a compromise that only required very little time and expertise from Aaron."

"And the hair is a custom colour but it's a permanent dye job," Evelyn added. "I'd say he might have to do a little touch-up in two weeks and then I'll come back for a full redo in a month, if he's still around."

Alex looked back at Aaron.

"What do you think? Happy with the look?"

Aaron gave him a crooked smile. "I like it. I might just stay this way."

They all laughed.

Later that day, Aaron approached Alex and showed him the iPad in his hand.

"I think I'm ready," Aaron said.

"You sure? You only get one shot at this a day."

"I'm sure," he said as he handed the tablet to Alex.

Alex brought up one photo at a time and intentionally went out of order in case Aaron knew the names by rote rather than by recognition.

Aaron never even hesitated. He not only matched every face to the name but had memorised each person's bio and relationship to Alex.

Alex exited the app and handed the iPad back to Aaron.

"I'm impressed." Alex smiled. "You did good. If you can keep your prejudices under control, I think you've got this nailed."

"What prejudices?" Aaron asked innocently.

"Good," Alex nodded.

"Wasn't there some talk of a boat ride once I passed the quiz?"

"Did I really make that promise?" Alex said with a straight face.

Aaron was about to give him some shit when he saw the beginnings of a smile start to form.

"You got me, boss," Aaron exclaimed.

As promised, Toni drove Alex and Aaron to the Santa Barbara harbour. They waited until dark and took a longer, less trafficked route to cut down on the chance of Aaron being spotted. It was unlikely considering that he was wearing a heavy boating jacket with a collar that rose up almost to his ears. On top of that, he was wearing a wool cap that covered his head right down to his eyebrows.

It was late and the marina was almost completely devoid of boaters and boat watchers. It was dark and the marina jetty lights were all motion-sensing, saving money and stopping light from disturbing the overnighters.

As they passed through a sturdy security gate, Aaron could see a few cabin lights dotted around the harbour but none of those boats were on their floating dock.

Aaron was used to seeing boats. Naples had countless marinas berthing everything from small speedboats to mega yachts. The ones they were passing looked to be in the 40-to-50-foot range. Nice but not what you'd expect for a superstar like Alex Cole.

As they neared the end of the dock, Toni pressed a black fob, and a single light came on at the end of the jetty. It illuminated a diagonal boarding gangway that was attached to one of the biggest sport-fishers he'd ever seen.

"What the hell is that?" Aaron asked too loudly then whispered the same question.

"That's *Lucky Dancer*. She's a Weaver 87," Alex replied. "They're hand-built in Deale, Maryland."

"It's beautiful," Aaron said as they neared the sleek dark blue hull. Its pearl white superstructure rose high into the night sky.

They climbed the gangway and stepped onto a massive teak-floored cockpit. Toni stepped up to the access door, unlocked it and shuffled Aaron through to the interior. Once all three were inside and all the window coverings were drawn, Toni turned on the lights.

Aaron gasped.

It looked like a luxury condo. Earth tone fabrics and dark woods produced a sense of comfort and elegance. Alex gave Aaron a quick tour of the 'below decks' as Toni went back outside. There were three cabins, three heads, a full galley and a dining room.

When Aaron was being shown the master suite deep within the yacht, a loud whirring sound suddenly filled the air. Moments later, a second similar noise joined the first, doubling the effect.

What the hell's that?" Aaron asked.

"Toni has turned on the engine compartment blowers. It clears out any gas fumes that might have built up since we've used her."

"Makes sense," Aaron quipped.

"Let me show you something really amazing," Alex said.

He led Aaron down another deck then went aft. He opened a white watertight door and switched on the overhead lights. Aaron stared in amazement at the huge engine compartment. Two massive diesel engines sat idle on either side of the access ramp. The sound of the extractor fans was almost deafening.

"This is amazing," Aaron concurred.

"You haven't experienced the good part yet," Alex grinned.

They stood there for a full minute.

"What are we waiting for?" Aaron asked.

"It'll just be a few more..."

His words were completely drowned out as the starboard diesel roared into life. Aaron had never heard anything like it. The noise was all-encompassing. It felt like you were a part of the machine, such was the powerful rumbling vibration.

Then the port engine awoke.

Aaron couldn't stop smiling.

"Ready for some fun?" Alex asked.

"More than this?"

"Much more," Alex replied with a wink.

"Then, yeah!" Aaron shouted back.

"You'll have to stay below until we've passed the breakwater. After that, Toni will come and get you and you can join us outside. Once we are out on the bay, nobody will be able to see you."

Alex left Aaron sitting in the main lounge as he went outside to help Toni prepare for casting off. The yacht was secured on the port side only, so it made leaving the slip easy. They released all four of the mooring lines except one at the bow and one astern. Alex climbed up the steps to the bridge and took the helm as Toni released the bow line then ran aft. As the tide gently angled the bow away from the jetty, Toni released the final line.

Alex gently applied a little throttle to the port engine and the ninety-foot yacht's nose eased to the right, safely distancing itself from its slip. Alex kept their speed to a minimum so as to not create too much of a wake within the harbour. Toni walked along the port side and hoisted the fenders up and into their chrome holders so they wouldn't be in the way once under full power.

Five minutes later, they cruised by the breakwater and Alex pointed the bow parallel to the shore. He put the massive engines in idle then signalled for Toni to free Aaron from his confinement.

Aaron stepped out onto the aft deck as Toni killed the interior lights. Except for the glow coming from the helm instrument panel on the deck above and the yacht's red and green running lights, they were in complete darkness. It took Aaron a few moments for his eyes to adjust, at which point he could make out the dark waters of the bay and the gentle curve of the shore lights.

"You ready?" Alex called from above.

"You bet," he shouted back.

"Then come up here and enjoy the view."

Aaron carefully climbed the metal rungs and stepped out onto the raised helm station. He couldn't believe how high he was, yet he noticed another ladder leading up to still another level.

"Sit here," Alex gestured to a beige helm seat right next to his. Aaron lowered himself into the swivel chair and stared with amazement at the instrument and controls that were splayed out in front of Alex. It looked like the cockpit of a plane. Six different LED multi-screens showed maps, depth, radar, sonar, weather and one even had split-screen views from four camera positions at the bow and stern.

"You see these throttles here?" Alex asked, pointing to two chrome-handled levers.

"Yeah."

"Good. When I say so, I want you to push both forward slowly until these two dials reach three thousand."

Aaron looked worried.

"Don't worry. You can't break them." Alex smiled. "How are we below, Toni?"

"All's good down here," he called back.

"Push 'em forward, Aaron," Alex instructed. "Slowly but firmly."

Aaron took a deep breath and placed his left hand over the two throttles. He was surprised at how easily they moved. He gave them gentle pressure and could hear and feel the diesels roar beneath him. The yacht responded instantly and started to gather speed. The massive bow began rising out of the water. Aaron looked at Alex in a panic and stopped adding throttle.

"It's supposed to do that," Alex shouted. "As we go faster it'll drop and go on plane."

Sure enough, as Aaron continued pushing the throttles forward, he could see the speed increase to 25 knots and the bow gracefully returned almost level with the dark water.

"Keep going," Alex shouted.

Aaron gave it more power and was stunned to see the speed climb to 50 knots. They were slicing through the black water sending plumes of phosphorescent spray roiling to either side of the bow. The boat was so heavy and well-built that even as they ploughed through a four-foot swell, it couldn't even be felt on board.

"Want to take the wheel?" Alex asked, shouting above the noise of the twin diesels.

"Sure," he replied, trying to sound blasé about it when, in fact, he was terrified of doing something stupid.

Alex stepped to the left but kept his right hand on the wheel until Aaron was in position.

"Slide on over," he shouted.

Aaron took the other man's place at the helm and took the wheel in a death grip.

"Hold it gently," Alex explained. "She's very responsive. Turn the wheel gently to port."

"What?" Aaron yelled back.

"Left… turn the wheel to the left."

Aaron turned the wheel too sharply and the boat heeled violently to port.

"Gently. You don't have to yank her around. Try it again, this time to starboard…right."

Aaron turned the wheel, this time with a gentle controlled action. The yacht's bow moved gracefully to starboard while hardly even heeling into the turn.

They stayed out on the water for over an hour. At one point, they seemed to be headed on a collision course with a rising full moon. Aaron felt almost emotional at the sensation of such power being in his hands.

"You should go back below," Alex said as they approached the harbour entrance.

He took back control of the helm as Aaron climbed down to the cockpit.

The docking was as textbook as the departure. Alex and Toni worked in perfect sync as they secured the yacht to the jetty. Aaron was surprised to then see the pair washing and hosing down the entire exterior of the vessel.

Once complete, they did a final walk around to make sure everything was stowed or tied down. Toni opened the access door and made sure that the lights were off, and Aaron was ready to sneak off the boat.

Toni descended the gangway first then Aaron followed closely behind. As the two made for the car park, Alex strode down to the jetty, but as he was about to step off the gangway onto the concrete slip, a wave rolled through the harbour. It suddenly lifted then dropped the yacht. Alex lost his balance and grabbed for the gangway safety cable. His feet went out from under him and he slid off the metal walkway. Alex had a firm grip on the safety cable, but his right leg scraped against a raised bolt at the base of one of the gangway's chrome stanchions. The metal cut cleanly through his skin.

Toni heard the commotion just before reaching the security gate for the slip. He and Aaron ran back to the yacht just as Alex managed to pull himself up and onto the jetty. Blood was streaming through a jagged tear in his trousers.

"Call an ambulance then take Aaron home," Alex said trying to keep his voice low.

"I have to stay with you," Toni insisted.

"Not this time. No one can see Aaron. Get him out of here!"

Toni called 911, but instead of leaving immediately, he helped Alex tie a strip of his torn trousers around his thigh to act as a temporary tourniquet.

As he and Aaron reached the SUV, they could hear an ambulance somewhere in the distance.

10

CHAPTER

Doctor Peter Eisner was on duty in the ER. He was five hours into his second shift and was already feeling the effects of a double. It had been a long day, but Santa Barbara didn't have anything like the volume of emergency cases that he'd become used to in Los Angeles at the Freemont Hospital in Inglewood.

Freemont had been a war zone, and, after only six months, he realised that he couldn't take even one more day of treating victims of the ever-escalating gang wars.

On one particular shift, eight shooting victims arrived at once after a young punk managed to shoot up a neighbourhood with a knock-off AR15. He had apparently been aiming at a group of lowlifes gathered on a front stoop in Watts but managed to miss them all, and instead, pierced the cheap wooden siding of three homes on the same street.

He'd succeeded in shooting eleven innocent people. Two were dead at the scene and two died before they could even be triaged. He and the other two doctors on duty that night saved all but one of the remaining victims. That one was a little girl of seven. A 5.56 NATO round had gone through her living room window and had struck her in the neck while she watched a re-run of the Simpsons.

Peter had done everything in his power, and maybe even a little beyond that, to try and save the young child. She died on the table at 11:07 in the morning.

Peter gave in his notice at 11:56 that same day. He was contacted soon after by Bayside Hospital in Santa Barbara. The GM at Freemont had notified them that Peter, like so many before him, needed to walk away from the unending tsunami of gunshot victims but was still a great trauma doctor. Bayside had a much smaller staff than Freeman and had been short an ER physician for over six months.

The pay was less than Peter was used to but the trade-off with not having to deal with bodies ravaged by hot fragmented lead was a no-brainer. Two years later, he was exhausted but happy. Usually, he never had to pull a double at Bayside, but his night partner was in Hawaii on his honeymoon which left Peter as the sole trauma specialist in the town's only ER.

Peter's cell vibrated and he saw that he had a leg trauma patient inbound from the harbour area. He prepped the team and the moment the ambulance backed up to the ER entry, two nurses wheeled the patient towards one of the emergency room treatment bays. Peter looked at the amount of blood that had drenched the man's legs. Peter called for a blood-type cross-check as he was pretty sure the guy was going to need at least a unit or two, then had his team standing by in case they needed to prep the patient for surgery.

When Peter looked up from the wound to ask the patient a few standard questions, he recognised Alex Cole immediately. His face was drawn and pale but unmistakable.

The doctor was a big movie buff and a fan of action films, especially those starring Alex. Celebrities were not supposed to get preferential treatment but having one of the biggest film stars in the world on your gurney was bound to change the balance of care a little bit.

As they wheeled him into the first available bay, Peter took Alex's hand and told him that he would try and leave as small a scar as possible.

"Thanks, Doc," Alex said, sounding a little woozy from the meds the paramedics had given him. "Though, I rarely have to show off my legs on camera anymore."

"Just a couple of quick questions," Eisner asked. "Any allergies to any medication?"

Alex shook his head.

"Are you on any prescription medication?"

Again, Alex shook his head.

Alex was released just after dawn. No surgery had been needed. The paramedics had applied butterfly sutures which had allowed the blood to begin the clotting process before they even reached the hospital. He had needed fifteen stitches in total and his calf looked like something from a horror movie. His leg bruises had produced an astonishing kaleidoscope of colours that ranged from dark purple to a sickly shade of yellow. The temporary stitches were starkly visible against the paleness of the skin surrounding the wound.

Doctor Eisner advised Alex that he needed to keep his leg up for at least a few days. He also needed to be prepared for the colours to intensify still further before his calf returned to looking like something a little more human.

Even in a relatively quiet town like Santa Barbara, word had been leaked to the media that Alex Cole had been injured and was being treated at the local hospital. The front entrance of Bayside became besieged by paparazzi and local news teams. Toni had seen the chaos and coordinated with the staff to permit him to collect Alex from the facility via the underground staff parking garage.

Toni left the black Range Rover back at the house and instead, brought his own hi-mileage Ford Explorer for the pick-up. Alex lay in the cargo area covered by a black blanket as they emerged from the parking area. A few pro-active cameramen stood vigil off to one side of the exit hoping to capture some good shots of the big star trying to sneak away. They were so focused on looking out for either a limo or at least some sort of luxury car that they hardly gave a second glance to an old Ford being driven by a Hispanic male.

Once back at the house, Alex became the centre of much sympathy and attention. Maria was almost beside herself when she saw the injury. Linda was sympathetic, but, at the same time, gave Alex a mild reprimand for having thrown caution to the wind and gone to the boat in the middle of the night. Aaron was concerned about Alex but was also straining everyone's patience with endless questions about what the accident meant to his situation.

Thankfully, Diana drove up from Thousand Oaks as soon as she heard what had happened and became the voice of reason within the house. She managed to calm everyone down and assigned each person specific tasks and responsibilities.

The hospital had provided a loaner wheelchair to help Alex get around the house until he felt comfortable enough to use crutches. He wasn't happy with either option and within a few hours of getting home, had gotten out of bed and hobbled all the way to the living room. Linda and Diana tried to persuade him to at least baby himself for a few days, but their words fell on deaf ears.

Alex was too pumped up about planning the identity gag against Cindy Snow. He doubted that Aaron could fool her for very long, if at all, but if he could dupe her for even a few seconds, the gag would be a success.

Alex spent the next few days focusing Aaron's training on all things Cindy. He was going to need to not just know everything about her, but also how the two interacted and spoke when around each other. Cindy and Alex had an almost verbal shorthand that had grown out of the endless hours they spent on the set of *Days and Nights* waiting for shots to be readied.

As Alex schooled him on Cindy, Aaron kept asking why he'd never dated her considering they had been, and remained, so close.

"You've just answered your own question," Alex replied. "We have been best friends for over two decades. We are closer than any married couple. We love each other, but not sexually. She's more like family."

"That's crazy," Aaron exclaimed. "You two could have been the perfect match for each other."

"We are a perfect match. That's the whole point," Alex explained.

"But you never had sex," Aaron stated.

"No, we didn't. We didn't need to. We are both happy with the way things are."

Aaron just shook his head in confusion.

"If I may say so, you put way too much emphasis on sex," Alex said. "You can get sex anywhere. Some will be good, some not. The thing is that friendship is different. One that lasts a lifetime is unique. That's what you should be striving for in life."

"If I may say so," Aaron mimicked. "Only someone who could sleep with any woman on the frigging planet would say that."

Their discussion was interrupted by a knock on the door. Aaron opened it.

"The nurse is here to change your dressing," Linda advised Alex.

"I'll be right there."

"Would you like me to get you the wheelchair?" Aaron asked with a straight face.

Alex gave him a fake scowl then managed to get up on his good leg as he reached for the crutches. With newly learned skill, he twisted himself through the office doorway and swung himself down the corridor.

Aaron was bored. There wasn't going to be any more instruction that day and he was sick of watching movies in his room. He knew he couldn't go anywhere near the front of the house because of all the gawkers who had gathered at the gate hoping to get a glimpse of Alex.

He wandered out to the back part of the property which was completely shielded from public view. There was one place he had yet to explore. Tucked away from the main house was a single-storey structure that had been built in the same Mediterranean style as the villa. Aaron was pretty sure it was a garage of some sort, but when he'd asked Alex about it, he was told to stay away from there.

The building was about sixty feet long, dissected by five ten-foot diameter arches. Each housed a black metal garage door. Aaron checked to see if any would open by hand, but none would. He found a secure-looking door on the far side of the structure, but it was locked. The top half of the entry consisted of a reinforced glass window insert, but a roller blind inside was pulled all the way down, so he couldn't see a thing.

Aaron circled the rest of the supposed garage but couldn't find any other access. He did, however, find an industrial-sized compressor unit for an air conditioning system. It was connected to the building and was on and running. He was dying to know what was inside. Making it the one place that he wasn't permitted to see or even discuss had turned the urge to know more into something insatiable that festered away in his brain.

He didn't like mysteries.

Aaron returned to the side door and was trying to peer around the side of the blind where there was a razor-thin gap.

"What are you doing?" Toni asked as he approached the garage.

"I just wanted to see what was in there," Aaron replied, smiling.

"That's Mister Cole's private place. Nobody goes in there without him."

"I bet you go in there," Aaron winked. "Don't you, Toni?"

"Only with permission and I know that you don't have that," Toni stated flatly.

"I don't want to go in," he lied. "I just want to know what's inside."

"If Mister Cole wants you to know, then he'll tell you himself."

"Don't be such a dick," Aaron replied. "I asked you a simple question and you treat me like I'm some sort of employee here. Well, guess what, Antonio? You're the employee around here. I'm a guest."

"You're an idiot," Toni replied, shaking his head as he turned to head back to the main house.

"You don't want to cross me, little man," Aaron called after him.

Toni kept walking.

11

CHAPTER

Diana drove through the front gate of Villa Miranda after having to wait for a newly acquired rent-a-cop to make a path through the throng of fans and reporters. They had laid siege on the house ever since the accident.

"Why won't you go down there and at least thank them all for their concern?" Diana suggested as she walked into the living room. "Once they see that you're in one piece, the media will hopefully start to lose interest."

"I'm not going to let them see me on crutches," Alex insisted. "That image of me would end up as either a meme or as the basis of a character cameo on the Simpsons."

"I wasn't aware the Simpson's producers had any intention of having you be a character on the show," Linda mentioned as if in passing.

"Don't rub it in. I mean, Christ, they've done everyone else."

Aaron stepped into the room.

"I couldn't help hearing your conversation," he said. "Can I make a suggestion?"

"*May* I make a suggestion," Alex corrected him.

Aaron rolled his eyes and carried on.

"Why don't you let me go down to the gate and be you?"

"Out of the question," Alex snapped back. "You're not ready."

"I've been ready for days," Aaron insisted. This is a no-brainer. It's not as if any of them know you personally. I would be this side of the gate so nobody would even be that close. I would just go down there, thank them, then walk back up to the house."

Alex was about to argue when Diana spoke up.

"I think it's a great idea. The whole reason we brought Aaron all the way out here was to fill in for you at public appearances. This would be a public appearance and he's ready…"

Alex started to scowl.

"Don't pull that face," Diana interjected as she playfully punched his arm. "You said yourself two nights ago that he was sufficiently prepped so let's try him out."

"What about my limp?" Alex asked defensively. "I can't just stroll down there as if nothing happened."

"I'm pretty sure I can fake a limp," Aaron replied.

"Let's work on that for a bit, and, if we all agree that it looks acceptable, Aaron can have his big debut," Diana suggested.

Three sets of eyes stared hopefully at Alex.

"Oh, for Christ's sake…alright. But Aaron—no ad-libbing. We will agree on your dialogue and you will stick to it. Is that clear?" Alex said with thinly veiled reluctance.

"Crystal," Aaron grinned. "What am I going to wear?"

Peering through slats in the den's plantation shutters, everyone in the house watched as Aaron walked down the drive towards the entry gate. He had a slight limp that was subtle and believable.

The mass of humanity on the other side of the gate pushed and shoved to get the best view through the filigreed wrought iron of the barrier.

Aaron stopped a few feet from the crowd. He had never been so scared in his life. This was a moment he'd fantasised about. He wasn't in some hick town doing an impression of Alex Cole. For the next few minutes, certainly as far as the crowd was concerned, he *was* Alex Cole.

He briefly closed his eyes and forced himself to relax. He had this. It was no big deal.

Aaron extended his right arm and waved at the gawking hordes.

"How is everybody doing?" he asked in perfect Alex Cole. He exuded confidence and warmth.

The throng all shouted back different responses, but all carried the same theme. They wanted confirmation that he, Alex Cole, was okay.

"You probably heard that I had an accident down at the harbour a few days ago. I wish I could call that fake news, but the fact is, I did. I tried jumping from my boat to the dock just as a wave swept through the harbour. I still made the jump, but my leg got a little scratched up on the landing. As you can see, I'm fine. There have been no ill effects and I am still on schedule to start shooting my new movie, *Hell After Dark,* in just over a month."

"Can we see the scar?" a paparazzi shouted as he tried to get his camera lens between the curved metal bars of the gate.

"Sorry, folks," Aaron laughed. "I have a rigid no-nudity policy and that goes for my legs as well."

Some members of the crowd laughed, others booed and moaned hoping for the big-dollar picture of the actual wound. The gorier the better.

"I'd like you all to do me a huge favour and go back to getting on with your lives and allow me and the others in the house some privacy."

Even as he spoke, uniformed police officers began mingling with the crowd and gently ushered them away from the gate.

"Leave the cute girls behind, officers," Aaron added. "I might be able to find a use for them later."

He then turned and walked back to the house.

"What the hell was that?" Diana said the moment Aaron walked through the front door. "You had a specific script. Why in God's name did you have to add the last part about the girls?"

"Because that's what I would have said if I was Alex Cole," Aaron shot back.

Alex and Linda joined the others in the entry hall.

"But you're not Alex Cole. You're a hotel manager from Florida," Diana replied as she shook her head in disbelief.

"That you brought all the way out here to be Alex Cole. That's what I'm doing," Aaron insisted.

Just as Diana was about to give Aaron both barrels, Alex stepped in.

"Why don't we all just calm down and start over. I think Aaron did a great job out there. I didn't like the little ad lib at the end either, but I'm sure we can put that down to stage fright. Isn't that right, Aaron?"

"Sure, Alex. It was definitely just a case of nerves."

Diana watched Aaron as he spoke and was certain she saw a momentary flash of anger flit across his eyes.

Four days later, the nurse removed the stitches from Alex's leg and pronounced him fit and able to walk sans crutches. He decided that it was time to go back to Los Angeles and carry out the prank on Cindy. Alex felt that Aaron was as ready as he was ever going to be, and with the TV publicity interviews coming up the following week, it was time for the big test.

Linda decided to stay at Villa Miranda and work on her latest painting. The return to LA was coordinated so that Toni would drive Alex to the city the next morning. Maria would then drive Aaron, covertly, to the West Hollywood house a little later in the day.

Maria had hoped to have a nice conversation during the ninety-minute drive, but Aaron flipped his hoodie over his head and went to sleep before they even pulled onto the 101 freeway. He didn't stir until they turned off Sunset Blvd and headed north into the West Hollywood Hills.

It was the first time Aaron had seen the LA house. When they pulled up to a plain stucco wall with a wooden electric gate in the centre, he wasn't particularly impressed. Even when the gate slid open and Maria drove through and he could see the house, he was still disappointed.

From the outside, it looked to be a single-storey wood and concrete rectangle with few windows and zero charm.

"I was expecting something a little more impressive for a big star like Alex Cole," he said, shaking his head.

"So, you're saying you don't like the house?" Maria asked trying to keep a straight face.

"I was hoping for something a little more dramatic, that's all," Aaron replied.

Maria pulled into the garage and waited until the electric door was fully closed before letting Aaron out of her car. Alex's black Range Rover was parked next to them and a pristine vintage Mercedes 450SL had the next stall. Aaron was surprised to see that there was still room for another car beyond that. From the outside, the garage hadn't looked anywhere near big enough.

Maria opened a plain white utility door and held it open for him.

"Let's go, Mister Peterson. I'll show you the unimpressive film star house."

The immediate interior did nothing to change Aaron's opinion of the home. They were in a utility and laundry room. The washer and dryer were big and expensive-looking, but the room was plain white and lined with wooden shelves and cupboards.

Maria saw the look on his face and shook her head as she opened another door and they stepped into the house proper.

The white room led to a spectacular kitchen. Rich amber-flecked granite surfaces contrasted with hand-made cream-coloured cabinetry. A central island was bigger than Aaron's entire apartment in Florida. Maria led him to a set of dark wood swing doors that opened into the living room and dining room. The décor was modern, comfy chic.

It wasn't the plush furnishings or the floor-to-ceiling black slate fireplace that stunned Aaron. The space had to have been sixty feet long and one entire wall was made of frameless folding glass doors. Beyond that was a dark teak-covered patio surrounded by an immaculately tended lawn that bordered an infinity pool. Its water appeared to stop in mid-air, high above Los Angeles. The regimented north/south boulevards of the city seemed to fan out from the hillside like an art class example of diminishing perspective.

The day was surprisingly clear for Los Angeles, and Aaron could see not just the Pacific far off in the distance, but the cluster of islands that were nestled off the coast as well.

On the far left of the back area, cleverly shielded by living bamboo trees, was the guest house. Maria opened a sliding door and gestured for him to go inside. What Aaron hadn't realised from the outside was that the guest house had been cantilevered out above the steep hillside. There was a living room and bedroom beyond, both of which had floor-to-ceiling tinted windows that gave one the impression of being in the cockpit of a plane as it descended prior to landing.

Even the bathroom had one wall of nothing but glass looking down at the urban sprawl. The architect had cleverly used electric frosting glass. Though it was nice to be able to look down at the rabble far below, one didn't necessarily want them to be able to look up and see you in your most private moments.

Aaron was fascinated by the technology. Just by flipping a switch by the bathroom door, the wall of glass instantly became opaque. He'd seen something like that in a few movies but had assumed it had been a digital effect, not an actual thing.

"Still disappointed?" Maria asked sarcastically.

"I spoke too soon," Aaron said with what sounded like real humility. "This place is gorgeous."

"I think the expression is—don't judge a book by its cover," Maria winked at him. "You get settled in and come into the main house when you're ready."

Maria let herself out.

Aaron kept his humble smile right up until the door was firmly closed.

Then, the smile vanished. He didn't like being told what to do, especially by someone's maid.

12

CHAPTER

Later that day, after one final rehearsal, it was time to pull off the big prank. Alex and Aaron stepped into the garage. Alex hesitated for a moment then led him to the convertible Mercedes.

"I never thought to ask," Alex said as they reached the car. "Can you drive?"

"Just because I'm not really Alex Cole doesn't make me some sort of moron. Of course, I can drive."

"Relax, Aaron. I'm just checking. I want this to go perfectly. You should drive and I'll do the hoodie routine, okay?"

Aaron looked lustfully at the pristine sports car.

"Absolutely."

"Good. Remember, no speeding, no attention-seeking—just blend in."

"Can we at least put the top down?"

Alex was about to respond when he saw that Aaron had been kidding.

It was dusk and some of the lights in the other homes on the narrow, hill streets were already on. They reached Sunset and Alex told him to turn right. Aaron loved the feeling of driving the powerful car down one of the most iconic streets in the world. Once, a car pulled up alongside them at a traffic light and the driver obvious saw and recognised who was behind the wheel. Aaron gave the gawking woman an ultra-cool head nod then pulled away.

Alex directed him to take the right fork at the Doheny Drive intersection, then, after a few hundred yards, turn right again onto North Hillcrest. They pulled up to an impressively large gate which opened immediately after Aaron gave his best Alex Cole impression into an intercom.

The house was just visible at the end of a sweeping driveway. Lit by reproduction carriage lamps, Aaron thought it looked like a southern mansion rather than the Hollywood home of a film star. With its white-pillared frontage, it immediately reminded him of *Tara,* the plantation house in *Gone with The Wind.*

Aaron stopped the car before getting to the end of the drive so that Alex could slip out and wait in the shadows. The front door of the house opened as he pulled up in front of two of the columns. Cindy appeared. She was smiling, framed by the golden light from inside the home.

Aaron felt his pulse rate quicken as he stared back at the girl of his dreams. If anything, she was more beautiful off camera. Her features were somehow more subtle than when viewed through a camera's eye. He already knew every pixel of her face. For over twenty years, he'd sat inches from his television studying her. Worshipping her. He knew exactly how her jade-coloured eyes reacted to light. How her right pupil had just the slightest dark flaw that only appeared in direct sunlight.

Aaron stepped out of the car and up the front porch steps. She gave him her iconic grin that showed her cheek dimples to perfection. The fact that he was climbing the stairs of a Tara-like mansion to embrace his personal fantasy heroine made him feel, just for a moment, how Rhett Butler must have felt climbing similar steps to be with his Scarlett.

It wasn't what he and Alex had planned but Aaron decided then and there that the moment needed more than just a few words of greeting. Cindy deserved more than that. Aaron stepped towards her with the intention of grabbing her around the waist and spinning her as if they were dancing. Before he could step close enough, an oversized black German Shepherd galloped out of the house and stopped beside her.

Something about the way the animal was staring at him made him freeze in place.

The dog growled and his ears went flat.

"Buster?" Cindy laughed. "It's Uncle Alex. What's the matter with you?"

Aaron offered his hand as a show of peace, but, after one sniff, the dog resumed the growling.

"Well, that's a little odd," she laughed. "So, what was so urgent that you had to get off your death bed and come down to LA just to see me?"

"Hardly a death bed," Aaron replied as Alex Cole. "It was just a bad scrape. Everyone's made it into such a big deal."

"Tell me about it!" Cindy replied. "When that shithead I was living with slugged me in the face a few years ago, all I got was five lines in the LA Times. Two stitches and a black eye and I get one lousy paragraph, and that was buried on page eleven. You scratch your poor little leg and I have to hear about it on CNN."

Aaron was trying to stay in character, but Cindy had knocked the wind out of him. She had lived with another man. He'd never heard anything about that. He never even knew that she'd ever had that serious a relationship with anyone. That was not part of the fantasy at all. Aaron had always thought of her alone, waiting for the right man. Him. Now, everything was going oddly off-kilter. There was a nagging thought that was hammering to get into his head no matter how hard he tried to keep it at bay.

Cindy was no longer clean.

No longer virtuous.

No longer a virgin.

"I guess that shows which of us is the biggest star?" Aaron tried to joke, though inside, he felt as if a nest of spiders had moved into his stomach.

"Don't get me started," Cindy scoffed. "Your stuntmen should be the ones with their names on Hollywood Boulevard. In every single one of your movies, fifty percent of your screen time is someone else pretending to be you. The day you decide to make a movie that doesn't involve explosions and crashing helicopters, then we can start comparing careers."

Aaron felt the blood rushing to his head. Alex had briefed him on the banter that the two indulged in, but even knowing that couldn't stop him from feeling a burning rage simmering inside.

Aaron momentarily forgot what Alex had told him about how he and Cindy always somehow got into it over women versus men in Hollywood. He'd been told that it was all in fun, but Aaron felt his face redden as she practically scolded him.

He didn't like being scolded.

He hadn't liked it as a child, and he didn't like it now.

He still still felt sick inside when he remembered the day that his mother had had one too many of her lunchtime Martinis and had

Aaron had to shake off the memory. He was a grown man now. He was Alex Cole and was standing in front of Cindy Snow.

He realised that he was being an idiot and that he still desperately wanted her even if she had chosen to have a relationship with someone else at some point in her life. The fact was that, although he still loved her, he recognised that he now couldn't help thinking of her in a slightly different way.

The news of her having lived with another man, plus the disrespectful way she had just berated him, had obviously changed the dynamics of their relationship. Cindy was no longer the innocent girl next door that she portrayed in her films. Aaron now saw that she needed a strong influence to put her in her place and teach her how to respect her man. After all, if there was one thing he'd learned growing up in Florida, it was that you don't let your woman talk sass at you.

"You are such a bitter old crone," Alex stated, laughing as he stepped out of the shadows.

Cindy did a perfect on-stage double-take. She looked from Alex to Aaron then back.

"What the fuck is going on?"

Alex stepped up onto the porch and leaned over Buster. The dog raised his ears and began to wag his shaggy tail. He moved forward and slowly rolled onto his back exposing his tummy. Alex gave him a vigorous rub.

"Why don't we go inside, and I can explain," Alex suggested. "You should know that you have just helped my friend Aaron here to graduate from the Alex Cole school of mimicry and impressions."

"You ass," Cindy said as she shook her head and stepped inside. "Shame I never fancied you, Alex, otherwise, with two of you in my house, this night could have turned into something weirdly kinky."

Alex laughed. Aaron did as well but his mirth was fake. This woman who he'd loved for so long and to whom he'd remained spiritually faithful, was crude and vulgar. She wasn't anything like the girl he'd carried next to his heart for over half of his life.

Aaron realised that it was going to take much more stick than carrot to bring Cindy back into line.

13

CHAPTER

Alex decided that he wanted to do the driving on the way back and that Aaron would be the one donning the hoodie.

"You went a little off-script back there," he pointed out.

"She was so completely different from what I expected," Aaron replied.

"That's always the case when you meet someone famous. The public always expects at least some of their screen persona to exist in the real person. What people refuse to understand is that each role that an actor plays is different. The character is different, the dialogue is different. It's all just make-believe."

"But she was so different," Aaron insisted.

"You weren't listening to me when I told you that she was nothing like the woman in all those romantic comedies, were you?"

"I heard what you said, but still thought that…I don't know. I guess I still thought that she'd be funny and gentle and…cute."

"She is funny and gentle and cute, just not like her characters," Alex stated. "Would you seriously prefer the movie Cindy over the real one?"

"I like the girl in the movies," was all Aaron could manage.

"Aaron, you never stop amazing me. Her characters in those films were so one-dimensional. Don't you want someone with depth? A woman who will challenge you. Someone who has their own opinions and isn't afraid to defend their beliefs. Doesn't that sound better?"

Aaron turned and looked directly at Alex.

"No."

Alex was about to respond when he had to suddenly slam on the brakes. He had been pulling away from a traffic light when someone stepped in the path of his car.

"Get down," Alex shouted as he pushed Aaron further down in his seat.

A paparazzi hoping to catch some rappers pull up in a half-million-dollar supercar had been hovering outside the Sultan Club on Sunset Boulevard. When he spotted Alex Cole driving the Merc, he jumped in front of the moving vehicle as he raised the camera.

Alex only just managed to stop before striking the guy with the car bumper. Police officers in a West Hollywood cruiser on the other side of the street gave their siren a single whoop and the paparazzi scurried back to the sidewalk. As Alex started to pull away, the man held out his hand like a gun and pointed it towards Alex's head.

Alex kept driving but saw in his mirror that the police had seen the gesture and had pulled a U-turn in the middle of Sunset. They jumped out of their vehicle and were confronting the photographer. He knew that he should stop but was all too aware that if he did so, Aaron would be seen and the whole plan would be a bust.

He did the next best thing. He called Larry from his car and told him what had just occurred, especially the part about the mimed gun.

"I'm at the Bristol Farm Market on Beverly. I can be there in less than two minutes," Larry said before ending the call.

Alex doubted that the paparazzo was anything more than an opportunistic asshole trying to score a high dollar celebrity photo, but the gun gesture had freaked him out. Obviously, if the man had wanted to kill him right there on the street and had been armed, he could have. That's what had unnerved him the most. All the plotting and subterfuge to get Aaron ready to fill in for him and then he puts himself in a position where anyone could have shot him dead.

Alex made up his mind that until his shooter was found, he was going back to complete isolation and would let Aaron be the target as originally planned.

The next morning, when Diana texted a viral photo of Alex looking startled behind the wheel of the car, she had added one single word of text.

"You?"

He replied with one word. "Yes".

"Why?" she texted back.

Before he could even start to type a response, his phone rang.

It was Diana.

"Please tell me why you are paying a fortune to have a body double cover for you, yet the first thing you do when you get back to town is cruise Sunset?" she asked.

"We were coming back from Cindy's after Aaron's test run."

"How did that go?"

"It went well. He fooled her completely."

"Did he behave?"

"Almost," Alex replied.

"That still doesn't explain why you didn't have Toni drive you both in the SUV with the nice tinted windows so nobody could see you," Diana said.

"I thought the Range Rover would stand out," he offered somewhat lamely.

"So instead, you took a bright white, vintage Mercedes convertible? Makes perfect sense to me."

"Let it go, Diana," Alex said. "I learned my lesson. I'm a hermit from now on."

Diana's voice softened. "I'm glad to hear it. Let the kid get shot; that what he's getting paid for."

"Now, now," Alex chided. "By the way, did you hear from Larry last night? He was going to check in with the police at the scene."

"He called after you turned your phone off for the night. The guy was scum, but harmless. Being detained by the police scared the hell out of him."

"He wasn't scared enough to not sell the photo," Alex commented.

"He thought he was being clever doing that finger gun gesture you used in *Shark Tooth*. Apparently, he thought you'd find it cool," Diana added.

"I want this to be over. It's bad enough being stalked by fans. Having to worry if one of them is armed is just too much. Did Larry happen to mention whether the police have anything new to report on my shooter?"

"He did and they don't."

"Sorry about last night," Alex conceded.

"I know you are. Just for God's sake keep your head down and stay safe."

Alex disconnected the call just as Aaron crossed the back patio from the guest house.

"The guy last night was harmless," Alex said as Aaron stepped inside.

"I saw the photo online. You can't make out my face at all. I'm in shadow," Aaron sounded disappointed.

"That was the idea," Alex reminded him.

Aaron shrugged then headed off to the kitchen to grab some breakfast.

Diana arrived at the house just after two. When she walked through the front door, she saw two Alex Coles. They were dressed identically. She walked between them and entered the living room. She turned to observe the pair as they followed her in.

Diana smiled and walked up to one of them. She kissed him on the cheek.

"Nice try," she said.

"How the hell did you know?" Alex asked.

"Your clone forgot to limp."

Aaron sighed and bowed his head.

"Shit," he mumbled.

"I wouldn't worry about it. Most people don't expect me to be limping anyway," Alex offered.

Diana wished she could have just told him she would know the real Alex Cole out of a hundred clones. She knew every strand of hair, every slight imperfection.

Of course, she did. She'd been in love with him since high school.

There'd been a few times when she had almost plucked up enough courage to tell him how she felt, but every time, something somehow derailed her.

The worst period had been after Miranda died. Alex was a complete mess. One night, he'd been drunk—very drunk -and had kissed her. As he led her to his bedroom, she felt euphoric but at the same time knew that he was using her simply to fill a void. She pulled away and forced him to drink coffee and unload the tangle of painful and confused thoughts that were spinning around inside his head.

Instead of making love to Alex, Diana had stayed up all night with him as he poured out the bile and darkness that had moved in once his wife had lost her valiant battle with cancer.

At one point, Alex's head had been on her lap as he sobbed with unrestrained emotion. Diana stroked his hair and had helped him through that awful night, all the while, feeling herself drop farther into her own lingering pain.

Alex only once mentioned their having come scarily close to becoming lovers on that night. It was almost three months later, and they were in the middle of a budgeting meeting, when Alex, out of the blue, asked her why she hadn't gone to bed with him. She told him that she wasn't going to be a rebound romance, plus the fact that she worked for him. She pointed out that sleeping with the boss never ended in the plus column.

Alex hadn't responded to her comments; instead, he had nodded his understanding and acceptance of her words.

"What if you didn't work for me?" he asked.

"If you're serious, let's talk about this once you've gotten Miranda out of your system with somebody else and are serious about it."

"Have you two gone over the questions I sent earlier?" Diana asked, snapping herself back to the present.

"A hundred times," Aaron replied.

Diana didn't miss the irritation in his voice.

And if the host goes off script?" she asked.

"I say that I'd prefer not to discuss that," Aaron answered.

"No ad-libbing on these shows. One wrong comment and I have to spend a week putting out fires."

"I know," Aaron shot back. "I heard you the first hundred times."

"Oh, this is going to be fun," Diana said, shaking her head.

"It's just nerves," Alex commented.

The drive to KABC studios in Los Feliz took much longer than it should have, as an accident on Sunset impacted all eastbound traffic in Los Angeles. Diana had tried to engage Aaron in some lightweight conversation, but he remained moody and quiet.

"What's bothering you?" Diana asked as they crossed over Highland Boulevard.

"You tell me!" he replied bluntly.

"I honestly have no idea what you're talking about," she responded.

"Why do you dislike me so much? I mean, what the hell have I ever done to you?"

"Aaron," Diana began. "it's not that I dislike you, it's just that I was hoping you'd be more of a team player in this little project. Instead, you seem to make everything about you. The thing is that nothing that we are doing is about you. It is always one hundred percent about Alex and that's it."

"What does that make me?" Aaron countered.

"It makes you exactly what you are. An employee. You were hired for a specific job. All we want is for you to carry out your instructions like anyone else would. We're not here to fuel your narcissism every minute of every day. In a few weeks, you will be back in Florida with a healthy bank account. In the meantime, stop feeling that Alex owes you in some way or that you deserve any part of his celebrity. All you have to offer is a resemblance and the ability to mimic. There is only one Alex Cole, and you are not him."

She turned to see his reaction. Sensing her look, he turned and smiled back at her.

"You're right," he said, sounding surprisingly sincere. "Sorry for being such a douche. I'll do better."

"Thank you for understanding," she replied.

Diana was relieved to get an apology. However, she wasn't happy about what she'd seen in his eyes. With the contacts in, they looked like Alex's except there was one glaring difference.

She'd never seen Alex look at her with such raw hatred.

14

CHAPTER

"Do you ever wish there could be one more movie in the *Deadly Recourse* franchise?" Marta Chu asked. "I know the audience would love to see just one more film."

As if on cue, the audience erupted with cheers and applause.

Aaron smiled back at the afternoon TV host and waited for the crowd to settle down. Under the intense illumination from the broadcast studio lighting, Marta Chu looked nothing like she did on TV. She was older and her cherubic facial features, which Aaron used to think made her look exotic and sensual, looked almost bloated under a heavy coat of stage makeup.

"I would be the first one to raise my hand if the studio asked the cast if we wanted to do number six, but I somehow don't think that's ever going to happen," Aaron answered almost apologetically.

"But why not?" Chu pushed. "You heard my audience. Everyone would love to see one final movie."

"Marta, I think it's a story problem rather than an unwillingness to add to the franchise. My character did die at the end of the last movie," Aaron replied in an amused tone.

"But did he?" Chu asked in an overly conspiratorial voice.

"I died in an explosion at a nuclear power plant. The audience saw me get vaporised."

"But did they?" she asked with the same 'maybe I know a secret' attitude.

As Aaron looked at her pudgy features and lacquered hair that looked to have the softness of a football helmet, he wanted to reach across and slap some sense into her. He'd already said no, and she just kept on at him.

Diana was standing at the back of the studio feeling as if she was about to bring up her pitta bread and hummus lunch. Chu had managed to back Aaron into a corner. She wanted him to parry with her. Aaron had not been trained to verbally spar with a professional. Diana could sense him starting to get angry and could do nothing but pray that he could hold on just a little while longer.

"I'll tell you what, Marta," Aaron said with a warm smile. "If you and your audience can persuade Global Studios to reincarnate my character for one more outing, I promise you that I will bring my character back from the dead and make the picture."

Aaron then turned to the crowd.

"You heard it here first, ladies and gentlemen," Aaron held out a hand, gesturing to them. "If you can convince the studio, then I'm in! Call them. Email them. March up to the studio gate! It's in your hands now!"

The audience went nuts. They whooped and cheered like there was no tomorrow. Aaron managed to spot Diana at the back of the studio and gave her the subtlest of nods. She responded by giving him a slow clap of thanks. She wasn't crazy about him suggesting that his fans storm the studio battlements, but he'd certainly taken control of the interview.

Over the next ten days, Aaron took part in five local talk shows and one syndicated program. His performances on camera became more relaxed and natural. By the end of the local interview cluster, he was able to laugh with the hosts and even deal with left-field questions that were not part of his rehearsed repertoire.

While Diana was pleased with his newfound confidence, she couldn't help but notice a cockier side to his personality off-camera. She wanted to discuss it with Aaron, but with only one local show left to do, she didn't want to knock him off his stride.

The next host should have been an easy one. Dave Tucker was the film reviewer for the NBC affiliate and had always had a soft spot for Alex. There was a feeling of mutual respect between the two and Diana had no concerns that Dave would go easy on him.

The interview on the set of *Movies Now* started in a normal friendly way. Tucker kept the questions easy and on topic. Aaron had no trouble keeping the exchange upbeat and collegiate. Then, just to keep things interesting for the audience, David asked a slightly off-topic question. It wasn't unusual nor was it remotely aggressive. Alex would have hit it out of the park.

"Let me ask you a question as more of a friend than an interviewer," David said. "You reached that scary age of forty not too long ago. When I first interviewed you fourteen years ago, I asked you if you were still going to be making action movies when you turned forty or whether you hoped, by then, to have moved to other genres that were maybe a little more cerebral. Do you remember what you said?"

Diana, who was sitting among the audience, wasn't in the least bit fazed by the question. In fact, she thought it was a good one, one that she herself had asked Alex on a number of times. She remembered the show when Dave had originally brought it up.

"Well, Dave, I am over forty and am therefore allowed to not remember every word I uttered that long ago."

Dave laughed. "I'm lucky in that I have access to the old show library. Want to see how you responded?"

"More than life itself," Aaron replied with false sincerity.

The screen above and behind the set faded from the Movies Now logo to the set as it had looked fourteen years earlier. Both Dave and Alex looked younger.

The old video zoomed to a closeup of Alex.

"If I am still jumping out of perfectly good buildings and blowing up helicopters when I am forty, I want you to personally put me in a straitjacket and ship me off to the nearest recovery centre for narcissistic actors."

The present-day audience laughed as Dave reached behind his seat and produced a straitjacket and held it out to Aaron.

Aaron gave Tucker a big smile, but Diana could see immediately that it held no warmth whatsoever.

"Well, Dave, let me put it this way," Aaron replied while making no move to take the offered prop. "I make on average about twenty to thirty million per picture before residuals and ancillary markets. What do you make? I'm just curious."

Tucker was clearly surprised by the question, but he was a pro and knew how to step over the obstacles.

"A hell of a lot less than that," he laughed.

"Have you ever been a film star yourself, Dave?" Aaron asked.

"Why no, I haven't, Alex." Tucker didn't like the question or the way it was asked.

"Then, may I suggest," Aaron began, "that you do not ask me personal questions about my choice of roles? Maybe when you become a star and start earning some decent money, you and I will have something to talk about. But, until such time, you should stick to being a critic and leave the film-making to the big boys."

Diana felt the studio spin around her. It was like watching a train wreck that just kept on ploughing through building after building. She was trying to get Aaron's attention but then he managed to find the perfect way to plunge the locomotive right off the cliff.

"We have a saying about film reviewers. 'People who end up as film critics are the people who can't find any other way to be in show business.'"

Aaron then stood up, removed his lapel mic and walked off the set.

Tucker looked directly at the camera and said, straight-faced, "We have a saying too. 'Those who can't take the heat really shouldn't come near this kitchen again. I think it's time for a commercial break.'"

The audience were still in shock at seeing Alex Cole melt down right in front of them. Eventually, one person started to slowly clap Tucker's handling of the event. Soon, the entire audience was giving him their applause.

David Tucker had won them over.

Diana caught up with Aaron in the parking lot.

"What the fuck was that?" she shouted.

"That was Alex Cole not appreciating that bullshit question."

"No, it wasn't," Diana shook her head. "That was a petulant child having a tantrum on television. Dave Tucker is a friend of Alex's.

There was nothing incendiary about that question or his little gag. In fact, I liked it. It was a funny bit."

"Then next time, you can sit up there and have some B-lister ask you a bunch of dumb questions," Aaron shouted back at her. "Oh wait. You can't because nobody gives a shit what you have to say."

"And you think that people care about what Aaron Peterson has to say? They don't! You know why? Because you're nothing. You're a nobody."

"Fuck you. I'm Alex Cole."

"But you're not. Your just some guy doing an impression. That's all."

"That's not all. I know I'm not really Alex but when I'm on a TV set talking to a host, I am Alex Cole to everyone in the studio and everyone at home."

"That doesn't give you the right to show everyone insecurities that Alex Cole doesn't even have," Diana said, trying to steady her voice. "Do you have any idea what it's going to take to repair what you've done here today? Do you?"

"No, and I don't care. Someone had to knock that guy down a few pegs," Aaron insisted.

"What pegs? There were no pegs. David simply asked you a question and you lost it."

"Look, I just wanted to…"

"I don't care what you wanted," Diana snapped. "Please just get in the car."

Aaron begrudgingly obliged, but not before being accosted by three young female fans who wanted selfies with their favourite star. Diana watched as Aaron posed for one-on-one pics with each of them then a group shot that each wanted taken with their own phone.

The three girls giggled as they walked away while comparing photos. Diana shook her head in dismay. Despite the meltdown, she still had to admit that the guy did a good Alex Cole.

<h1 style="text-align:center">15</h1>

CHAPTER

The return drive was even more strained than the trip to the studio. Aaron was in a deep sulk and glared out of the passenger window the entire way back to West Hollywood.

When they arrived at the house, Alex and Martha Hess were waiting. Word of the debacle with David Tucker had already reached them. It was unusual for Martha, as a studio head, to get involved with something seemingly so unrelated to film production. However, with principal photography expected to start for *Hell After Dark* in just a few weeks and the advance media packs all ready to be released globally, she couldn't let one supposed tantrum from the star upend the whole promotional strategy.

"Aaron, would you mind excusing us while we talk about you behind your back?" Alex said, trying not to sound overly prosecutorial.

"I fucked up pretty bad, didn't I?" Aaron asked.

"On a scale of one to ten, I'd say you probably hit a nine point five. We're going to talk on the back patio, so why don't you wait in the den and watch a movie or something?"

"Okay," Aaron replied.

Alex studied him for a moment.

"It might not be so bad. Just give us about half an hour."

It took much longer than that.

An hour later and the four were still scheming outside as Aaron tried to focus on an episode of *Air Crash Investigations,* one of his favourite shows. He couldn't care less about the forensic investigation and astounding detective work that was needed to find the cause of each of the accidents. He just liked the digital re-enactment of the crashes themselves.

Especially the ones involving lots of flames.

Aaron fully expected to be fired. He couldn't believe that he'd lost it like that. He loved being Alex Cole and wasn't yet ready to stop. As he watched members of the NTSB crash investigators test a theory about the crash in a wind tunnel, he started to feel anger rising to the surface.

Aaron knew the sensation. He'd had it for as long as he could remember. Before he'd found ways to keep the raging fury in check, he was constantly getting into trouble for fighting or just plain trying to hurt people. Watching someone else in pain was the only thing that helped relieve the sensation inside.

As he got older and realised how vital it was to keep the anger concealed, Aaron found ways to calm the fire before it fully took hold. He'd tried meditation and even yoga, but though mildly effective, neither was able to extinguish the raw heat.

The one thing that worked every time was for Aaron to focus on sex. Strangely, it was not sex driven by anger or a need for pain. Instead, he liked to fantasise about gentle, almost romantic lovemaking. Maybe it was because such a ritual was unachievable for him. The few sexual encounters that Aaron had experienced were not in the least bit gentle. The girls…there had been only three in his life, had been paid for and the sex had been violent and unfulfilling.

Aaron turned off the TV and closed his eyes. He began to run the same footage that always calmed him.

He thought of Cindy.

He imagined them both walking back to their room at a lavish hotel. They were arm in arm and ecstatically happy. When they entered their luxury suite, Aaron turned Cindy to face him, then kissed her gently on the mouth. She returned the kiss. At first, their lips were hesitant and searching but soon passion took over.

Aaron started to unbutton Cindy's black silk dress…

The sound of the front door opening knocked Aaron out of his fantasy dream. He knew that Maria and Toni had gone out to Whole Foods to stock up the kitchen and the others were on the patio where they wouldn't be able to hear the new arrival.

Aaron got to his feet and immediately felt his erection straining against his linen trousers. He made a quick adjustment so that his dick was pointed up rather than down and felt instantly more comfortable.

"Surprise!" Linda said as she threw her arms around him as Aaron walked into the living room.

Aaron was about to tell her that she was hugging the wrong man, but there was something about the feel of her against him that derailed any such rational thinking.

He kissed her neck.

"It feels to me like you're happy to see me," Linda said as she felt his bulge pressed against her.

Aaron was too shocked by the situation to say anything.

Linda moved her hand down and cupped his erection.

Aaron felt the room spin. Feeling her grasp his cock sent a wave of sensations throughout his entire body.

Suddenly, Linda pulled away and stared into Aaron's eyes.

She looked confused.

Before he knew it, she pulled up his right trouser leg and saw that there was no trace of the recent injury. Aaron was about to apologise when she slapped him so hard that he stumbled against the hallway wall.

"You disgusting little pervert. If you say one word of this to anyone, I will fucking cut off your tiny little prick and force it down your throat."

Aaron heard one of the sliding doors to the patio open.

"Everything alright in here?" Alex asked. "Linda! What a lovely surprise. I thought you were going to stay up in Montecito!"

"I was, then I realised that I was actually missing you and decided I couldn't wait to see you."

Linda walked into Alex's arms.

As Aaron headed back to the den, Linda kept her eyes riveted on him. He'd never seen a woman so angry before.

"Aaron," Alex called out. "Don't go anywhere. We've finished our little chat about you. Want to join us on the patio so we can put this little mess behind us?"

"Sure," Aaron replied as he took the long route to get outside, thus avoiding getting anywhere close to Linda.

"What happened to your face?" Alex asked.

"I was just trying to slap some sense into myself," Aaron answered.

"Did it work?"

"I hope so."

"Honey, do mind giving us a few minutes? We're just finishing something up," Alex asked.

"You do what you have to. I think I'll make myself a nice big drink in the meantime," Linda replied.

Aaron slipped outside, but not before Linda managed to shoot him one last loathing glare. He took an empty seat at the glass-topped dining table and waited for the crucifixion to start.

"You are incredibly lucky," Diana began. "Alex spoke with Tucker minutes after you walked out. He told him everything; who you really were, why we had hired you, and the damage it could cause if what we were doing was to get out. Tucker was relieved. He had been agonising over what he could have possibly done to upset you so much."

"He's agreed to not air that show," Alex added. "We're lucky that *Movies Now* is recorded for air the next day. I had to promise to let him re-interview me when all of this is over."

"What about the live audience?" Aaron asked.

"Tucker told them that I hadn't been feeling well all day and that it was suspected that I had food poisoning. Thankfully, the show has a strict no cell phone policy so we shouldn't have to worry about any of the interview going viral."

"What can I do?" Aaron asked. He actually sounded humble.

"The West Coast interviews are finished, and the late-night shows aren't scheduled for two weeks," Diana stated. Hopefully, by that time, we won't need your services any longer."

It took a moment for her words to fully sink in.

"Are you saying that I'm not fired?" he asked.

"Alex persuaded us that since you were already here and were fully trained to be Alex, it would be counterproductive to cut you loose while the shooter is still out there," Martha offered.

"That said," Diana jumped in, "one more episode like today and you are gone, and in case I have to remind you—so is the $20,000 bonus payment."

"I know," Aaron nodded. "It won't happen again."

"There's only Comic-Con in San Diego on Saturday and the charity auction the following Thursday," Alex advised. "I was thinking that maybe on Sunday we could head back up the coast and work from Montecito?"

"That sounds great," Aaron replied as if he meant it, which in this case, he did. "I like it up there."

"Good, then that's settled," Alex replied, smiling.

Martha was the first to go as she had a late meeting on the set of what should have been a simple low-budget film. The problematic young director seemed to be channelling *Michael Bay* as he kept trying to turn the adaptation of a simple mystery novel into an effects-driven action adventure.

Diana was the next to leave. As she headed out, Linda caught up with her on the driveway.

"Are you free for lunch tomorrow?" Linda asked.

"I could move some things around. Any specific reason?"

"I want to talk to you about something that's bothering me," Linda said as she lowered her voice.

"Something to do with the new member of our family?" Diana asked.

"I don't want to talk about it here. How about Laurel Hardware around noon?"

"Sure. Text me the reservation time and I'll see you there."

"Thank you," Linda said then turned back to the house.

"Is this something I should be concerned about?" Diana asked.

"Of course not. I just need to say a few things. Anyway, it would just be nice to have lunch together and catch up."

Linda gave her a smile and a wave, but Diana wasn't buying it for a second. After the meeting, she'd felt some heavy tension between her and Aaron and had wondered what the guy had done this time.

She desperately hoped there wasn't going to be another fire she was going to have to extinguish.

16

CHAPTER

Diana arrived early at the restaurant and was able to get one of the prized outdoor tables. By a second stroke of luck, the Los Angeles weather didn't seek to burn, blow or gloom away the al fresco dining experience. Thanks to a gentle breeze coming in from the Pacific, the terrace temperature was a balmy seventy-eight degrees.

Linda arrived exactly on time and was clearly impressed by Diana's seating coup.

"You must know people," Linda joked.

"I do. I know you," Diana replied.

Though neither usually drank at lunchtime, a visit to the Laurel somehow wasn't complete without one of their signature Caipirinhas. While waiting for their cocktails to arrive, Diana reached across the table and took her friend's hand.

"What's going on?" she asked.

"I'm probably just overreacting," Linda said.

"Overreacting over what?" Diana pushed.

"Aaron. There's something off about Aaron."

"I agree that he's certainly not someone I would add to my Christmas list, but you need to be a little more specific."

"I keep catching him staring at me," Linda stated.

"You're a beautiful woman," Diana said. "That can't be an unusual occurrence."

"Thank you," she laughed. "But he doesn't just look at me like a man checking out a woman. I can't describe it but it's as if he's…"

"Undressing you?" Diana suggested.

"More like ravaging me."

"Yuck," Diana replied.

"Isn't it strange that someone can look exactly like the man I love yet can make my skin crawl just by staring at me? When he first arrived at Villa Miranda, I caught him watching me when I was doing my yoga out by the pool. I can't be certain, but I think he may have been touching himself."

"Oh shit," Diana voiced.

As I said. I don't know for sure as he was partially hidden behind the living room curtains," Linda added.

"That makes it even more creepy." Diana grimaced.

Linda was about to continue when their drinks arrived. After a quick toast and glass clink, she continued.

"Yesterday, when you were on the patio talking about Aaron, I came through the front door and momentarily thought he was Alex. I put my arms around him."

"Oh Jesus," Diana gasped.

"He hugged me back and I still thought it was Alex. The clothes and even the aftershave…"

"He'd just come back from doing the David Tucker interview. He was supposed to be Alex," Diana explained.

Linda looked uncomfortable as she took a big sip from her cocktail.

"When I pulled him close to me, I could feel that he was aroused so I stroked him."

Diana lowered her head to her hands.

"I then knew immediately that he wasn't Alex," Linda said as she stared down at the linen tablecloth.

"Should I ask how?" Diana said in almost a whisper.

"Let's just say that there's much more to Alex than meets the eye. The same cannot, however, be said for that little perv."

"What did you do?"

"I slapped him as hard as I could," Linda stated.

"And…" Diana asked.

"It felt wonderful."

"I meant—how did he react?"

"Like a big baby," Linda said, brushing aside an errant hair from her face. "I actually thought he was going to cry. It was pathetic."

"Unfortunately, I think that pretty much describes Aaron to a tee," Diana agreed. "I have to assume that you haven't told Alex about any of this?"

"No. I know that he'd fire him on the spot and though I can't believe I'm going to say this, we actually need the little shit."

"What can I do to help?" Diana asked.

"You're doing it right now," Linda said. "You're being my friend and listening to me. No one else knows about any of this and it has to stay that way. I just wanted to talk to someone and make sure I wasn't going crazy."

"Not at all," Diana said shaking her head. "Maybe us bringing a complete stranger into our home is the crazy thing. Would you mind if I shared this conversation with Larry? I think that he may want to double-check the reports he got on Aaron from the people who did the background check."

"As long as nobody else hears about it, I'm fine with Larry knowing. If anyone in this town can keep something confidential, he can."

"What about you?" Diana asked. "Are you going to be okay with Aaron being in the house?"

"Yes and no. I'm driving back up to Villa Miranda in the morning, so, that pretty much tells you how I feel about being anywhere near to him."

"What about when Alex and Aaron head up there at the weekend? You're going to run into him at some point."

"It's a big piece of property," Linda replied. "I'm sure we can find a way to distance ourselves. If not, that little shit better not try anything, or his balls will be the next target."

"He might just like that," Diana mentioned.

"Not if I use garden shears."

Larry was concerned when he got the call from Diana about some strange behaviour from Aaron. Larry had never had cause to find fault with any of the reports from Somerset Fields Investigations. They were one of the largest private investigation firms on the planet and were, usually, overly thorough.

He called his contact with SFI and was put through immediately.

"Larry! How are things in the land of Democrats and earthquakes?" Terry Singleton asked from his office in DC.

"They're good. I'm just following up on the Peterson guy your people looked into."

"You must be reading my mind," Terry said. "I just got the final report in an email less than half an hour ago. I just finished it and was about to forward it to you."

"I hope it was as innocuous as the preliminary one?" Larry asked.

There was silence from the other end.

"Terry?"

"Yeah…basically, not much else came to light except that, since sending you the prelim, the team were able to speak to a few people who have known Peterson for a while, including when he was a kid. The new report also contains material from Peterson's records that weren't initially available."

Larry felt the same unease he used to feel when was a detective and things were about to go sideways.

"What else was there?" he asked.

As you know, in Florida, a background check only shows convictions, not arrests, which are expunged automatically if charges are not formalised. It turns out that our boy has been picked up a few times. Plus…"

"I don't like it when there's a plus."

"Sorry, but you know it's not unusual to dig up a few turds when we're able to spend more time on a background review," Terry said. "Anyway, we did find that the guy's got a juvie record, but it's sealed."

Why didn't we know that after the initial background check?" Larry asked. "They should have shown up even if we couldn't get access to them."

"I agree," Terry replied. However, we weren't aware of a name change at that point."

"Excuse me?" Larry blurted out.

"Aaron is not his birth name. He was christened Brian Peterson and had it changed to Aaron shortly after his parent's death."

"Reason?"

"Nothing obvious unless he wanted to distance himself from the juvie stuff, but as they're sealed anyway, I don't see the point."

"What's your thinking?" Larry asked. "Could there be something that needed hiding?"

"We don't know. Could be anything. We know his parents died in a house fire. There could be psych evaluations, treatment records…who knows. Juvenile records are always sealed and basically off limits."

"What about the adult records?" Larry asked.

"As for the arrests, we know approximately when they occurred but don't have any of the details as to the reason or the charges. Florida likes to protect the innocent."

"Innocent?" Larry asked sarcastically.

"Again…we're talking about Florida. Innocence is graded on a curve down there. If you want, I can have the team shake some more trees and see what falls out. That's the one good thing about the Sunshine State. Personal privacy can be bought and sold like a commodity."

"Send me the report and I'll read it on the plane," Larry advised.

"Where are you going?"

"Florida. Ask the team to stay in Naples for one more day. I'd like an in-person debrief."

"When are you leaving?" Terry asked.

"Now."

17

CHAPTER

Larry had read the sixty-two-page report by the time the Gulf Stream crossed over New Mexico. It was more detailed than the interim one but there was still nothing that showed Aaron as being a danger to Alex and the others. That said, there were also a few areas that needed fleshing out.

The expunged adult arrest records were definitely going to be the easiest targets. Larry knew from experience that Juvie records were always harder to obtain than the adult equivalent, plus they could also unearth a treasure trove of issues that might explain later-life behaviour.

Diana stopped by Alex's house to let him know that Larry was back in Florida doing some final due diligence on Aaron's background report. Normally, she would have just called to speak with him but with a highly skilled imitator in the house, she wanted to make sure that she was speaking to the real Alex.

"Where's Aaron?" she asked the moment Maria opened the front door.

"He's in the guest house," Maria replied.

Diana could tell that she was upset about something.

"I am looking forward to when he is gone," Maria stated bluntly then turned and headed for the kitchen.

"Maria," Diana whispered. "Why? What's he done?"

"I don't think I should…"

"If there's something wrong with Aaron, you need to tell me," Diana insisted.

"Everyone in this house always treats Antonio and me very kindly. All of the guests who visit do the same."

"Go on," Diana urged.

"That Mister Peterson…he's different. He's not a nice person."

Diana put an arm around Maria and led her into the utility room then closed the door.

"How is he not nice, Maria? I need to know."

Maria hesitated as if searching for the right words.

"He treats us as if we are less than him," Maria began. "He treats both of us as if he were our employer and doesn't really like who we are."

"Do you think it's possibly just because he's nervous and isn't sure how to treat you?"

"Maybe, but he keeps saying things like… *'maybe that's okay down in Mexico, but up here, we have standards.'*"

"He said that to you?" Diana asked in amazement.

"He says things like that every day…then there's…never mind." Maria shook her head.

"Maria, please finish what you were about to say."

"He plays tricks on us," Maria whispered. "He makes us think that he's Mister Cole and then laughs when he sees that he has fooled us. It's very scary sometimes how much like Mister Cole he can be."

"Yes, it is," Diana agreed. "Maria… I would like you and Toni to let me know the next time that Mister Peterson speaks down to you or tries to trick you. Do you understand?"

"I don't want to get anybody in trouble. We love working for Mister Cole and have never once complained about anything."

"I know you haven't. I also know that Mister Cole is very fond of both of you and would be very upset at anyone who treated you badly."

"Thank you, Miss Trent." She smiled.

Maria's mood seemed to have brightened slightly. Diana gave her a brief hug.

"Where is Mister Cole at the moment?" she asked.

"He's in his office," Maria advised.

Diana popped her head around the door of what had once been a bedroom, but Alex had converted it to his private office. The walls were lined with built-in bookcases which were filled with scripts, historical novels and an astonishing number of books on crime, both fiction and non-fiction.

"May I come in?" Diana asked.

Alex looked up from his leather-topped desk and smiled.

"Diana! I didn't know you were coming by," Alex said.

"I just wanted to have a quick word with you if you have a minute?"

"Of course, I do," he stated. "What's up?"

"Before we start, may I please ask a strange favour?"

"I guess so. Yes," Alex replied, obviously slight intrigued.

"Would you mind showing me your bad leg?" Diana asked.

"I always thought that they were both pretty good," he replied flippantly.

"I'm serious," she said.

"I can see that."

Alex hoisted his right leg onto the desk and pulled up his trouser leg. The healing gash from the accident was plainly visible.

"Thank you," Diana voiced.

"Anything else? Special password? Secret handshake?" he joked.

"I just needed to be sure that I was actually talking to Alex Cole."

"Is that really necessary?" Alex asked, mildly perplexed.

"Apparently, yes," she replied.

Diana filled him in on what Larry was doing in Florida as well as what Maria had just told her moments before.

"We just discussed Aaron yesterday," Alex stressed. "We all know that he's got some rough edges. Hopefully, by the time we have to go to New York, we will have paid him off and said a fond farewell."

"What if Larry finds something else about him?" Diana asked.

"Let's worry about that if it happens. I greatly doubt that that hotel chain he works for would have him managing…"

"Assistant managing," Diana corrected.

"Whatever," he continued. "They wouldn't leave him alone in charge of the hotel at night if there was anything even remotely questionable about his background."

"You could say the same thing about the *Bates Motel*," Diana jibed.

"That was different. It was family-owned." Alex grinned.

"While we're on the subject, I've got to ask you why you're giving this guy so much rope? You've always been fair with people, but, at the same time, you haven't been one to accept substandard work."

"First of all," Alex replied. "I'm not sure that Aaron has been giving us substandard work. He was hired to fool people into thinking that he was me. He's been doing just that. Also…and please don't ask me why… but I feel slightly guilty for how we're using Aaron."

"Why?" Diana blurted out.

"I spent some time yesterday evening looking at his videos online. There was something kind of sad about a guy whose only claim to fame is that he can do an impression of me. Not even an impression, really. He was able to look and act exactly like me. I can't explain it, but I feel kind of responsible for him."

"Oh, please!" Diana shook her head. "That is complete nonsense. There are thousands of people online doing very good impressions of you. That doesn't mean that you need to adopt them all."

"I'm not suggesting adopting anyone; besides, Aaron is different."

"How in God's name is Aaron different from all the others?"

"He's different because we brought him here. He lives with us. He actually knows something of what it feels like to be me."

"Because he's staying in the guest house?" Diana shot back. "I think you're over-analysing this."

"It's not just the guest house," Alex continued. "We flew him out here on a private jet. He's been with me on the boat. He eats and drinks with us. My God, we even showed him how to change his appearance and his voice so he could be exactly like me. Whether you want to admit it or not, he has been living a superficial version of Alex Cole's life."

"I love it when you talk about yourself in the third person," Diana joked.

"I'm being serious. We've created some sort of a bond."

Diana looked back at him with real concern.

"What?" he asked.

"I just hope we haven't created some sort of a monster."

18

CHAPTER

The Gulf Stream touched down in Naples as dawn's rising light cast a swath of pale orange across the Florida Everglades. Larry's rental car was waiting for him by the small executive terminal. His first stop was back at the Rancho Suites Motel. He wanted to be there just as the morning shift change took place. He was hoping to talk to some of Aaron's co-workers to see if any of them knew of any skeletons in the guy's closet.

Larry had time to grab a Denny's Grand Slam breakfast on the way there. He wasn't holding out too much hope for getting good info at the motel. If there was one thing he'd learned early on as a detective, it was that the truth was rarely just sitting there in plain sight.

One of Larry's first cases as a detective with Hollywood Robbery-Homicide had been what appeared to be a targeted murder outside a down-market strip mall off Western Avenue. He was partnered with an overweight and undermotivated detective who was only a few weeks from completing his twenty.

Though only fifty-three, the guy looked at least fifteen years older. Then again, each year of being a cop in Los Angeles seemed to count as one and a half years anywhere else, except maybe Chicago and Detroit.

Amos Fletcher didn't just look old; he was mentally burned out as well. He seemed to have no qualms whatsoever in accepting his pay without expending even a modicum of effort. Larry had hoped that his first partner would be someone who would at least be slightly motivational.

When they pulled up to the taped-off crime scene, Amos told him that he was going to stay in the car and that Larry should liaise with the patrol officers who had first arrived at the murder site.

Larry learned that the deceased was a known punk who made a habit of trying to shake down the customers and businesses of the strip mall and surrounding area. Larry looked at the body and saw that the man appeared to have been shot in the left eye. Only a small amount of blood had seeped from the deflated eyeball.

"Gunshot?" Larry asked the Medical Examiner who was just finishing off his notes.

"Small calibre if it was a gun," he answered. "Plus, if it was, it was far enough away to have not left any GSR."

Larry found the responding officer who told him that he'd heard from some of the locals that the owner of the mini-mart across the street had verbally threatened the victim on numerous occasions.

Larry reported the information back to Amos, hoping that that information would make the case a little more appealing to his lazy partner.

"Good. Then this one's a no-brainer." Amos smiled.

Amos told him to question the market owner, then detain him.

Larry didn't like the idea of labelling a murder investigation a no-brainer before either detective had spoken to even one potential witness. But, at the same time, he didn't want to be known as the rookie detective who refused to follow the instructions of a senior officer on his first call out.

He questioned the market owner, a balding, nervous Asian man who couldn't have weighed more than ninety pounds. Larry asked him directly if he owned a gun. The man proudly showed him a vintage-looking side-by-side shotgun. It didn't look to have been fired in more than a decade. Larry could see traces of rust inside the twin barrels. He worried that if the man ever did fire the thing, it was more likely to blow up in his face than stop a robber.

Larry returned to the car and informed Amos that he greatly doubted that the store owner was the shooter. Amos just shrugged and kept reading the paperback in his hand.

"Okay, big shot," he said. "If you don't want the low-hanging fruit, solve it your own way."

"Aren't you even going to help?" Larry asked, amazed.

"I already did, and you didn't want it," his partner replied. "Good luck, kid."

Amos wound up his window.

Larry had the two uniforms who had responded to the call check out all the other businesses in the mall. It was gone seven in the evening, so, apart from the mini-mart across the street, the other businesses were all closed. The officers returned within minutes and confirmed that all the premises were shut and locked tight. He asked the same officers to check all the dumpsters and trash cans in the immediate area.

Larry was about to report back to his uninterested superior when he noticed a man standing in the crowd of ghoulish onlookers. He was hard to miss. He was Asian, which wasn't exactly a surprise in a neighbourhood called Little Korea. What made him stand out was that he was well over six feet tall and was wearing a white doctor's coat with a logo that seemed to depict a pair of hands pressed together in prayer.

That rang a bell with Larry. He looked back to the upper floor of the L-shaped strip mall. A metal-railed, open-air walkway led to five businesses. A nail salon, a questionable-looking dentist and a Korean food store took up the long part of the L. The shorter part housed a tanning salon and what was, according to the signage, an acupuncture and aromatherapy centre.

Their logo was a graphic of a pair of hands praying.

Larry's eyes met those of the man in the white coat. The guy dropped his gaze to the sidewalk but didn't move. Larry stepped under the yellow crime scene tape and approached him.

"May I speak with you?" Larry asked.

The man slowly raised his head and nodded. Larry spoke to the guy for almost fifteen minutes. The man seemed pissed off about not being able to return to his business, but other than that, acted like any other onlooker at a crime scene. The problem was that Larry had this sixth sense that the guy knew more than he was letting on. He was trying to decide whether to bring the guy in for questioning when he heard his partner shouting at him from across the parking lot.

"Come on, numb-nuts. Let's go back in and squeeze this guy."

Much to Larry's astonishment, Amos had the mini-mart owner in handcuffs and was folding him into the back seat of their car. Larry ran over and stood close to his partner.

"It's not him," he insisted. "I can feel it."

"I'm glad you got feelings and all, but maybe after you've been a detective for more than five minutes, you might actually know what the fuck you're doing. In the meantime, when you got a suspect that everyone says had a beef with the victim, plus had a gun right there in the store…"

"That shotgun hasn't been fired in years and would have taken his head off if it had been used," Larry insisted.

"Who's talking about that old antique? I'm talking about this little beauty that Achmed here had in the cash register."

"My name is not Achmed!" the prisoner shouted from the back seat.

Amos ignored him and raised up a baggie that was holding a black Saturday night special with a duct-taped handle.

"Are you gonna get in the car with me so we can double-team this terrorist back at the station, or what?" Amos asked angrily.

"No. I don't think he's our guy. I want to stay here and check out a few things," Larry responded.

"You do that, and I'll be requesting a new partner," Amos shook his head. "Stop trying to be some sort of super-sleuth on your first time out. There'll be plenty of opportunities to grandstand, if that's your thing, once I've retired. For now, go with the flow. We question this guy, charge him, then we can go our own separate ways. Me, I'll be cuddling up to my good friend, Jim Beam."

"No," Larry stated. "I'm staying here."

Amos got back in the car, flipped him the finger then drove away.

Larry sighed and was about to return to the guy in the lab coat when one of the officers he'd sent off to search the trash appeared by his side. He was holding a sealed evidence bag up for Larry to see. Inside was a bundle of about twenty or thirty acupuncture needles bound tightly together. There was dried blood at the sharp end.

Larry looked back at the gawkers and saw that the man in the white coat was still there and had seen what the officer had found.

His eyes met Larry's as he nodded once.

Larry arrived at the motel a few minutes before seven. He wasn't scheduled to meet the investigative team until eight-thirty at a Starbucks on 5th Avenue, so had plenty of time to ask some of the staff about Aaron Peterson.

There were only two staff members ending their shift and three starting theirs. Larry quickly found that the two finishing their night's work were relatively new and had minimal interaction with

Aaron. The three who'd just clocked in, however, were far more promising.

Peter Harling, the daytime assistant manager, had been working at the Rancho Suites for over two years and had developed some strong feelings for Aaron—none of them good. Peter invited Larry into the motel's business office. It was little more than a ten-foot square windowless cube. It was filled with the cheapest functional office furniture that Rancho Suites had found to throw in there.

"Personally, he gives me the creeps," Peter said the moment Larry shut the door. "I don't know exactly how to describe it, but it was as if he didn't like people at all. He could be super nice and give everyone that big smile of his, but you could see in his eyes that he was hating every minute of it."

"Did you socialise with him at all?" Larry asked.

"Not really. The closest we came was when all the assistant managers in the East Coast division were invited to Orlando for a Rancho Suites management retreat. We were there for two full days, mainly stuck in a meeting room, but after each day's session, there was a big dinner and an open bar."

"Sounds like fun," Larry commented dryly.

"It was actually better than it sounds," Peter explained. "Everyone had a little too much to drink and told stories about their worst guest experiences. There was a lot of laughter and sharing. It was actually kind of cathartic."

"And Aaron was part of that?" Larry asked.

"Yes and no. The first night he sat with us and seemed to be enjoying it, but then the stories he told about bad guests suddenly started to get nasty and kind of dark. It wasn't so much what the guests had done, rather what Aaron told us he wanted to do to the guests. He seemed to feel that any of them that crossed him… those were his words... any of them that crossed him needed to be punished. He talked about cutting the brake lines on their cars or setting fire to their rooms. The more he drank, the more vindictive he sounded."

"Do you have any reason to think that Aaron may have actually carried out any of those threats?" Larry asked.

Peter shrugged.

"I never heard about anything happening to any of them. But after that weekend, when I saw that coldness in his eyes when he was talking to a guest, it gave me the willies."

The remaining two staff members had little to say that was of any use to Larry. One did complain that Aaron was very strict about timekeeping, but other than that, didn't seem to have any other opinions of the assistant manager.

Larry left the Rancho Suites at eight-fifteen and got to Starbucks with three minutes to spare. The two investigators caught his eye as he stepped into the over-chilled coffee house. Larry wasn't sure if the place was that cold or whether it was because he was stepping in from high heat and 99% humidity.

The two were seated at the far back of the premises where three armchairs had been shoved together around a low circular coffee table. The team comprised a man in his thirties who looked exactly like a poster boy for the FBI. He had a *Men in Black* quality, but without any of the charm. His partner was female, same age bracket, but looked more hardened by life than her counterpart. Larry guessed that she was an ex-cop and by the wear and tear he could see on her face, guessed her to have come out of one of the war zone precincts in one of the tougher big cities.

Larry could tell they were pros the moment he sat down. Instead of handshaking and other pleasantries, both produced their credentials before anything else was said. Though not requested, Larry did the same with his.

"How did it go at the motel?" Rita Myers asked.

"Not a lot of conversationalists," Larry replied. "Though one guy seemed to think that Mister Peterson had a dark side."

"Any proof of that?" Jason Pike looked as if he knew the answer before even asking the question.

"Of course not," Larry answered. "How about you two? Anything new since yesterday?"

"Not much as far as new information, but last night, one of the local cops asked me out," Rita replied. "I'd made him for a sleaze when I met him at the station. As I'd hoped, when we met up later for a beer, the guy drank too much and talked way more than he should have. Just around the time when he felt it was appropriate to start getting all touchy-feely, he let it slip that for the right inducement, he would be open to showing me the arrest records for Peterson."

"Sounds like a real charmer," Larry commented.

"I told him that I was very interested in his offer but wasn't into men. It took the idiot a while to get what I was saying, but when he finally did, he fumbled around trying to find a way to bring up money instead of sex. I told him that you were the money guy and would almost certainly be interested in striking a deal with him. If you're up for that, I'll text you his details."

"I have no foibles about bribing bent policemen." Larry smiled. "Was that true what you told him about not being into men? I'm only asking because if that was true, then my radar is on the fritz."

"I'll tell you what. Why don't you call my husband? If he's not too busy looking after our two kids, he can reassure you that your radar seems to be working just fine."

Larry laughed.

"Want to hear what I've got?" Jason asked. He almost sounded as if he was a little miffed at being left out of all the fun. "I spoke to an intern at the county courthouse and apparently, all juvie records are held right there in the City Hall building in good old-fashioned filing cabinets. All it takes is for someone to unlock the back storage room and look the other way for half an hour."

"You really can buy just about anything in Florida, can't you?" Larry offered.

"Everything except brains and low humidity," Jason fired back.

19

CHAPTER

Alex stood at the very edge of his property looking out over the lights of the city below. A mild Santa Anna wind had chased away the smog, giving Los Angeles an otherworldly and surreally clear appearance.

He'd spent the better half of the evening on the phone, FaceTiming with Codi, who was still stuck in Tokyo. He was finishing off the last leg of the press junket for his sci-fi feature, *Quantum Fire*.

Alex needed to hear his friend's opinion on Aaron's recent behaviour and whether Codi thought there was any danger in keeping him on.

"You're the ones that have to live with the guy, but as far as I can see, he's doing exactly what he's supposed to be doing. Sure, maybe he's got a little a prima donna thing going, but if I remember correctly, you went through the same thing the second they cast you in *Days and Nights*. Remember that trilby hat you bought thinking it made you look more like a star?"

Alex did remember the hat. He still had pictures of himself in the stupid thing. His favourite photo was one of him looking thoughtfully up at the sky with the hat rakishly tilted to the side. He recalled it as if it was yesterday. He'd thought he looked like a young film star who was wise beyond his years. In retrospect, Alex thought he'd probably looked more like a high school freshman hoping to get the part of Professor Higgins in a school production of Pygmalion.

Alex was the first to admit that he really had been a difficult little shit when he got that first part in the soap. The fact that he almost immediately developed a sizeable teen following hadn't helped to keep his swollen ego in check. Though he was unaware of it, people around him thought he was acting as if the world owed him a favour.

Then again, in some weird way, maybe it did.

Alex was raised in the town of Apache Junction, about forty miles outside Phoenix. His dad was a building contractor and his mother, an English Lit teacher in the town's tired and outdated middle school. Living in the back of beyond was cheap. They had a nice three-bedroom house on a third of an acre and even had a small kidney-shaped swimming pool.

They were basically living the reality of what was left of the American dream. They barbequed when it wasn't too hot and swam when it was. Pool parties were the norm in their neighbourhood. Though there was no formal roster, the local kids seemed to know whose pool to descend upon once Saturday rolled around.

Alex didn't have any plan back then in the summer of '92. Why would he? He was just a kid enjoying every minute of his life. He wasn't crazy about school, and his grades showed his reluctance to focus and learn. Many years later, his ADHD would be formally diagnosed but back in '92, it was presumed that he simply wasn't trying hard enough in class.

In the spring of that year, he was approached by Myrl Dicks, the art teacher who was directing the school play, to see if Alex wanted to try out for it. Alex had never even considered being in one of the school's productions. He had seen a few and thought they sucked. Plus, the kids he hung around with thought that anyone who had anything to do with the drama group had to be completely gay.

They were trying to put on a stage production of the movie, 'Stand by Me'. They needed someone for the role of Chris Chambers, played in the film by River Phoenix. Alex was torn. He didn't want his friends to think he was a homo but felt that if there was one actor that could never be considered a woofta, it was River Phoenix. Myrl managed to say the one thing that clinched the deal. He admitted that the only reason he was asking Alex to try out was that they'd run out of boys in the right age group that looked tough enough to play the part.

Alex agreed to read for it. Thankfully, he was blissfully unaware that the other reason that Myrl had chosen him was that he had always thought Alex to be a beautiful child and wondered how he would look fully made up and under theatrical lighting.

Alex soon found out that he had a knack for acting but seemed to find it almost impossible to learn his lines. By the second week of rehearsals, the rest of the cast were working off-book while he was still having to read almost every line from the scene pages. One of the other actors, the only black kid at the school, offered to help Alex not just remember his lines but also run through the scenes as often as he needed.

At first, Alex was a little concerned about accepting help from Paul. He knew his friends would give him crap for fraternising with the school's only black kid. Even though Phoenix may have become a multi-cultured metropolis, Apache Junction had not.

At the following day's rehearsal, Alex went out of his way to study what Paul was doing with his character. He was stunned to see the little nuances and inflections that Paul was able to add to his performance.

He also noted that the only way he was ever going to be able to give his role more depth was by knowing his lines inside and out. Without doing that, he would never give himself the luxury of exploring the inner workings of his character. He needed help but was more scared of the reaction of his friends than he was of not being able to act.

Halfway through one of the after-school rehearsals, a small dark-haired girl wandered into the auditorium and sat watching the kids on stage. Alex couldn't help but notice her. She was very boyish, but at the same time, kind of cute. She was also constantly twirling her hair around her index finger as she stared at the actors delivering their lines. As it got close to the point in the script when Alex joined the on-stage conversation, he suddenly felt completely embarrassed by being the only one holding the pages up to his face.

When he read his next line, he distinctly heard the girl laugh. This went on for the rest of the rehearsal. By the end, Alex was dreading every time he had to speak. He couldn't bear the thought of the cute girl laughing at him anymore.

The rehearsal finished on time at six. Alex grabbed his stuff and ran into the auditorium. He was astounded to see that the girl had left. He sprinted outside and saw her as she was retrieving her bike from the stand in front of the school building.

"Wait a minute," he shouted as he ran towards her.

She ignored him and continued extricating her vintage Schwinn from the rack.

"Why were you laughing at me?" Alex said as he stood blocking her escape.

"I was laughing at your character," she replied. "I love that he's always got a book up to his face. I think that's such a clever idea. It sort of makes him seem real and yet nerdy."

"I'm not trying to make myself look nerdy," Alex stated angrily. "That's not my character at all. I just have trouble with my lines."

"No!" she exclaimed theatrically. "I would never have known."

"You're making fun of me, aren't you?"

"Alex, you don't need any help looking dumb. You are managing that all by yourself having to read every line on stage," she replied. "Why don't you just do something about it?"

"What?" he snapped back.

"Learn your lines. You're good looking. You have a good voice, and even with the script blocking you from view, I get the impression that you might actually be able to act. Paul Waters told me that he offered to help you. Take him up on it, or else."

She pushed him aside with her bike and climbed on.

"Or else, what?" Alex asked.

"Or I'll keep coming to rehearsal and laughing at you," she said as she began to pedal away.

"I don't even know who you are!" he called after her.

"I'm Diana Trent, you goofball. I've sat behind you in history class all year."

He watched her cycle away then noticed Paul leaving the auditorium. He didn't even have to think twice.

"Hey, Paul. Can I ask you something?"

Alex and Paul became inseparable. Paul had shown him the secret to learning lines. When Alex first heard it, he thought Paul was joking. It sounded way too easy. The secret was to not just read the line and try to remember it. It was to understand the point of each scene and the reason his character says what he says. Paul filled in the blanks about who the character Chris Chambers really was, about his insecurities and his need to be accepted by the others. Paul took him through every single line on one particular scene and taught Alex to reach deep into his own experiences so that not only would the words have context, but they *became both real and memorable. By the end of their first session together, Alex was able to remember the entire scene they'd worked on.*

His friends unsurprisingly did just as he'd dreaded. They poked fun at him every time they saw him. Alex found that he could tune them out when they were just ribbing him. When they saw him and Paul together, however, their jokes grew nastier and more bigoted.

Alex found that the best way to curtail the ridicule was to avoid his old friends altogether. At first, that seemed to work, but after a few days, they started on an entirely new tack. They actively sought out the pair and turned up their verbal assaults to def-com 4.

One day, Paul and Alex stayed late after rehearsal to go over one particularly difficult scene. They were midway through the part where Paul's character is comforting Alex's.

"What a pair of faggots," Terry Ellis said as he and four others walked into the auditorium. Terry was a big kid even at thirteen. Naturally big-boned, his dad made him work most days after school at his tyre recycling centre. The manual labour had built strong muscles onto Terry's already large frame.

"Leave us alone," Alex said to him with forced calm.

"You can't tell me what to do," Terry snarled.

"Why don't you just leave us alone," Paul shouted at him.

Terry jumped up on stage and ran towards him, drawing back his right arm. Well defined muscle flexed in preparation for the punch that was on its way.

Paul raised his fists in a prizefighter stance, but Alex knew one thing that Paul didn't. Terry was a dirty fighter. The poised arm was just a misdirection while Terry used his foot to kick his victim where it hurt.

Alex stepped in and managed to unleash an uppercut just as Terry was parallel with him. It connected with his jaw with such force that they could all hear Terry's teeth smash together. He crumbled like a string-less marionette.

The other four ex-friends started for the stage when the air was shattered with a deafening siren.

They all turned (except Terry who was out for the count), and saw Diana standing at the back of the hall holding her personal anti-rape keyring alarm in her right hand. She walked to the front of the auditorium as the four would-be attackers held their hands over their ears.

She turned the siren off as she stepped onto the stage. She walked up to the biggest of the four, Simon Pope, and stopped only inches away from him. Though big, Simon was not even remotely fit. His size didn't come from carting hundreds of Firestone radials around a storage yard. His came from junk food and Big Gulps.

"What do you want, shrimp?" he asked Diana in his strangely high-pitched voice. "You looking for a little action?"

Diana slapped him so fast that he wasn't even sure he'd been hit, were it not for the ringing in his ears and the sharp pain on the left side of his face.

"What the fuck?" Simon cried. "I'm gonna…"

She slapped him again.

Simon didn't attempt another threat. Instead, he started to cry.

Diana turned to the other three.

"I think you're done here, don't you?" Her voice was low and menacing.

Gregg Harry, the runt of the litter, took a step towards Diana.

"You can't come in here and…"

Somehow, Diana managed to slap Gregg with one hand while activating her rape siren with the other. The sharp pain and impossibly loud sound coming from only inches from his ears were too much for him. He jumped from the stage and ran out of the auditorium.

"You should get your friend out of here," Diana stated, once she'd killed the alarm. "In future, I suggest you find yourself some other people to bully."

"But Alex is our friend," one of them declared.

"Was your friend," Alex said bluntly. "I don't need friends like you."

They somehow got Terry to his feet, though he seemed to be having trouble focusing his eyes. Despite his inability to stand on his own, they managed to help him down the aisle and out of the auditorium. Alex was about to thank Diana for interceding when the three heard a slow round of applause from a dark corner at the very back of the hall.

Myrl, the play's director, was sitting in the shadows giving them a slow hand clap.

"Fabulous," he emoted. "That, Mr. Cole, is how you need to play Chris Chambers. I want to see that you have that fire inside you even if your other demons are holding you back."

The play was a success. It ran for the full three-night schedule. A freelance entertainment critic who wrote primarily for the Phoenix Sun newspaper gave the show three and a half stars. He didn't make it a habit of attending amateur productions, but his nephew had a small part in the play, so he had to make an exception. While the play only got a so-so rating, Alex Cole's performance got the full five stars and an almost fawning review.

While nobody took the critique of a school play very seriously, it was intriguing enough to bring an LA casting director to the second performance. Petra Heel was being pampered at a highly exclusive Spa retreat only a few miles away when she saw the write-up. When she weighed the advantages of attending a high school play versus another evening of kale shakes and coffee colonics, she chose the show. She was glad she did.

Five minutes into the play and Petra was certain of two things; she never wanted to sit on a folding metal chair ever again, and Alex Cole was an extraordinary find. He was untrained, nervous and, on a few occasions, could be seen mouthing another person's dialogue leading into his own. None of that bothered her. She had seen far worse talent develop into serious actors. Besides, Alex had one ability that was the holy grail of acting. He exuded a sense of male sexuality without seeming to be aware that he was doing it.

Petra had studied first audition tapes from almost every TV and film star in America. As she sat in the overheated auditorium and tried to squirm some life back into her buttocks, she realised that Alex reminded her of a young James Dean.

It took Petra almost a month of phone calls and house visits to persuade Alex's parents to let her carry out a video audition. Usually, Petra had the candidate fly out to Los Angeles, but Mr. and Mrs. Cole refused to even consider such an idea, even when offered the chance to join him and stay in a five-star hotel. Instead, Petra booked time on a TV stage at the ABC affiliate in Phoenix.

She had told Alex and his parents that she didn't have a specific project in mind but wanted to be able to show his reel around town. Petra had lied. ABC was in pre-production on a new soap opera that was scheduled to begin airing later in the year. It was centred around a hotel magnate and his dysfunctional family. One of the roles in the new soap was for the troubled hotelier's youngest son—Jake Fallen.

The network had been pushing for existing young stars who had a history of working in fast turnaround programming. The problem was that most young talent used soaps as a steppingstone to a sitcom or even a prime-time drama. Few ever wanted to return to the daily grind of a five-episode-a-week schedule.

Thankfully, the director was a friend of Petra's and had agreed to check out her new find without the network knowing. Petra didn't tell

Alex that the script he was reading was from was an actual viable project and that he was, in fact, taking part in his first casting call.

She was surprised when, before they rolled the video, Alex insisted on knowing some background about his character. At first, she thought that he was just trying to portray himself as a real actor, but as she explained the horrid dynamics of the character's family, she could see his eyes light up.

He re-read his lines again to himself with a better understanding of who he was meant to be.

Petra called 'action' then delivered the first line of the scene. She was reading Jake's mother's lines, and the script called for her to sound drunk. When it came time for Alex's line, he kept his head down and, for a moment, Petra thought he'd frozen. Instead, Alex slowly looked up at the camera. A single tear hung from his right eye.

"You can't keep doing this to us. We're not one of your expendable boy toys. We're your damn family and we're not going to take it anymore. So, put down your martini, clean yourself up and start acting like our mother."

Petra felt a chill rise from her lower back and shiver its way right up her spine. For a moment, she thought that she was going to cry. She's never seen such understated power in a scripted delivery in her entire career.

Needless to say, Alex got the job.

Negotiations and concessions to the parents went on for almost two months. As far as his mom and dad were concerned, Alex wasn't going to give up school and simply run off to Hollywood just because some casting director said he was going to be famous.

Finally, all terms were met. Alex would be flown back to Arizona every weekend and while in LA, would be a full-time boarder at the famed Windsor Academy in Beverly Hills. He would be driven to and from the school only for specific shooting hours. It was a pain, but Petra and the network felt it to be worth the headache.

As a big PR stunt, the network announced that the first episode of Days and Nights *would be shot in front of a studio audience. As a surprise to Alex, his mother and father were going to be flown in so they could see their son tape the first episode.*

Fifteen minutes into the taping, Sheila Tapping, the associate producer of the show, stopped by the adjoining newsroom stage so that she could take a call. Her phone had been vibrating for five minutes. She knew the next-door stage was dark for the moment so she could finally have some privacy.

As she put the phone to her ear, she noticed something behind the news anchor desk. One of the backdrop live TV screens was showing breaking news. A private jet had crashed while trying to land in fog at Santa Monica airport.

As a sombre voice on the other end of the phone started speaking, Sheila felt the room spin.

20

CHAPTER

"Penny for your thoughts," Aaron said as he approached Alex. "You looked a million miles away."

Alex couldn't help but glance towards the lights of the very same Santa Monica airport where his parents had died that night. Usually, it was veiled in city smog or sea mist but because of the Santa Anna wind, the ILS runway approach lights were clearly visible even from ten miles away.

"More like twenty-four years ago," Alex replied.

"That was when your parents died, wasn't it?"

Alex turned to face him.

"Yes, it was. I don't know what brought that back tonight, but I guess it never really goes away," Alex reflected.

"I know how you feel," Aaron said. "It's been twenty-two years for me."

"Of course. I'm sorry. I was in my own little narcissistic world for a minute there. I'd forgotten that we have that in common."

"Sometimes it's good to share in another's misery," Aaron replied.

Alex wasn't sure exactly how to take that comment. Share in another's misery. That was one thing he never shared with anybody. It was way too personal and private.

"You know, I used to watch you every afternoon on *Days and Nights*," Aaron said. "You were amazing. Even on the episodes you did only a few days after their death, you were incredible. You had this inner light. It was if nothing could ever extinguish it."

"Those were the hardest weeks of my life. You only saw the few minutes when I was on camera. The rest of the time I was a mess."

"I know about that as well. I read about your drug problem and the suicide thing, but don't you think that all of that just made you better? Stronger?"

"No," Alex replied. "I don't. I think that had my parents not died when they did, I would be a far better person than I am today."

"I don't agree. It isn't until you have experienced true pain and had to survive on your own that you become complete and individual."

"Aaron," Alex used all his skills as an actor to not show the anger he was feeling inside. The death of his parents was a no-go area even to his best friends. To have Aaron try to convince him that their death had been a positive influence in his life was just too much.

"I'm a little tired tonight. Let's call it a day." Alex patted the other man on the arm then turned towards the house.

"I know that I became stronger after my parents died," Aaron said to Alex's retreating back. "Strong like you."

Alex felt the hairs on his neck do a little shimmy. He didn't know why. Yes, it had been a strange thing for Aaron to say, but then again, the guy was a little weird.

"Good night, Aaron," he said as he stepped into the house.

Aaron turned back to the view and stared across the city to the coast. He could make out the landing lights from Santa Monica Airport.

He raised his left hand and pretended it was a plane coming in to land at the airport. As it reached the ILS lights, he flipped his hand upside down and made the sound of an explosion.

Aaron closed his eyes and felt a wave of pleasure envelop his body.

Larry woke up early. He'd stayed the night at the Ritz Carlton overlooking Pelican Bay. It was one of his strict rules. When working on location for a client, stay somewhere nice. Larry didn't sleep well in cheap hotels where you could hear even the mice fucking.

His meeting with the bent cop Rita Meyers had told him about had taken place the previous night at a bar overlooking Rock Creek. Larry had been amazed when he saw the dump. In the first place, it wasn't a creek, it was a man-made harbour inlet that appeared to be where worn-out boats came to die. The water was black and topped with a sheen of gasoline and motor oil.

The Parrot's Perch looked as if it had once attempted to compete with Naples' popular tropical-paradise-themed shanty bars. The fake thatched roof and driftwood tables hadn't aged well. The building looked as if the next decent hurricane that blew through Southern Florida would erase it entirely.

The bar was empty save for one thickly set man sitting alone in a booth. His blue and gold Hawaiian shirt clashed with his blotchy red complexion. He saw Larry enter and waved him over. Larry could see immediately by the other man's exaggerated hand gesture that he was ploughed. He didn't mind that in the least. It saved him the trouble of having to get the guy drunk on his dime.

"Don?" Larry asked before slipping into the faux bamboo booth.

"Do you see anyone else here?" Don waved his hand horizontally around the room.

"Good point," Larry replied as he sat down.

Don looked towards the empty bar area.

"Can we get some fucking service over here!?" Don called out.

A Cuban man in his fifties stepped out from behind the bar's display wall of B-list spirits.

"How many times have I got to tell you, man…no swearing in here?"

Don brushed away the other man's comment.

"Who am I gonna offend, Mario? It's just you and me," Don slurred.

"What can I get you?" Mario asked as he slapped down a stained coaster embossed with the image of a grinning alligator. Beneath that were the words 'Elmo Beer; Take a Bite Outa Life'.

"What do you have on draft?" Larry asked.

"No draft in the off season. Too expensive to maintain the kegs."

"How about a Grolsch?" Larry asked, bemused.

"We got Bud, Coors or Millers,"

"How about a Corona?" Larry pushed just for the fun of it.

"Didn't I just say what we had?" Mario replied with bored exasperation.

"I'll have a Coors," Larry ordered.

Mario headed back to the bar.

"A cold one please," he called after Mario.

"Nice place," Larry commented.

"No, it's not," Don shot back. "It's a fucking dump but the beer is cheap and it's a private place to do business, if you know what I mean."

In a show of great subtlety, Don slapped his hand onto the table in front of Larry, palm up.

Larry stared at it as if not understanding the meaning of the gesture.

"Don't make me ask twice, dipshit. The hand's there to collect the money that bull dyke investigator promised me," Don growled.

"Oh, sorry." Larry feigned stupidity. "I don't know how this sort of thing works."

"It's pretty fucking simple, numb-nuts. You give me the money and I give you copies of the arrest records."

Larry reached into his trouser pocket and retrieved a plain white envelope. He placed it gingerly into Don's sweaty palm. After counting out the ten hundred-dollar bills, Don reached down and picked up a much-used manila folder from a cheap briefcase on the floor then handed it across the table.

"If there's anything else you ever need, feel free to get in touch," Don said as he pocketed the cash.

"There is something else that you could do for me," Larry replied as he flipped through the documents.

"You know my rate." Don grinned revealing nicotine-stained teeth anchored into pale, unhealthy looking gums.

"I'd like to hear your opinion of Mr. Peterson. You've been a policeman in Naples for over thirty years. Did you know him or at least know of him?"

Don did the same palm up routine on the table.

"I'll tell you what," Larry suggested. "How about you giving me your opinion of the guy as a courtesy between professionals."

"That's not how it works."

Mario appeared and thumped a bottle of Coors onto the coaster.

"Two fifty," he announced.

Larry gave the man three ones and a warm smile.

"Keep the change. The service was worth it."

Mario took the money and headed back to the bar. Larry distinctly heard him mumble under his breath.

"Pinga!"

"Let me put it another way," Larry said almost cheerfully. Give me your opinion and the recording of our little meeting tonight won't go viral. Does that sound fair?"

"Why should I believe that you've been recording me?" Don seemed confused.

"Jason, did you record all that?" Larry asked.

"Got it all Larry," Jason replied. His voice was crystal clear coming out of the cell phone in Larry's shirt pocket.

Don tried to lunge across the table. He was twenty years and a million beers too slow. Larry grabbed an outstretched arm, twisted it then lowered Don back into his seat before Don even knew what happened. He looked to be about to try another attempt at grabbing the phone when Larry spoke calmly.

"Don't make me hurt you, Don. Just answer the questions."

"Fuck you."

Larry removed the phone from his pocket.

"Looks like he's not going to go for it, Jason. Might as well upload the video."

"Video?" Don squealed. "No one said anything about a video."

"Oh, sorry. Yeah, there's a video as well. That's almost required nowadays to make sure something has the widest reach and best impact. A bent cop taking a bribe at a crappy bar in Florida is going to set the internet on fire."

"There's no way you could have shot no video through that shirt," Don stated.

"Jason, would you mind…?"

Less than fifty feet away, Jason's face appeared in the light of his phone. He was sitting on the unlit terrace beyond the restaurant's tinted glass windows.

Jason gave them a wave.

"Seen enough?" Larry asked.

Don nodded reluctantly. Jason turned off the phone light and the windows returned to revealing nothing but night.

"What sort of asshole would do a shitty thing like that to a brother lawman?" he mumbled.

"You ceased being a lawman the very first time you let yourself be bought. So…do we have a deal?"

"Will you at least buy me a drink?"

Larry slid his untouched bottle of Coors across the table.

"I'm a Bud guy," Don complained.

"If you don't want it," Larry shrugged and started to reach for the bottle.

Don may not have been that fast earlier, but he could move pretty well when he was rescuing a bottle of beer.

"So, what do you want to know?" he asked as he took a pull at his newly acquired brew.

"Just what I said before. I want to hear your opinion of the guy."

Don scratched at his thinning, greasy hair as his addled mind tried to recall any dealings he may have had with Aaron Peterson.

"Most of the time he was a nobody. But then, every so often, we'd get a complaint from some hooker or another that he'd got a bit rough. That's the three arrests in those files."

"Did he actually hurt the girls?" Larry asked.

"More like scared them into thinking he was gonna hurt them. The one weird thing is that all three girls said that he pretended to be that actor…shit, you know the one. The guy from Deadly Recourse. Alan somebody. No…Alex. That was it. Alex…?"

"Cole?" Larry suggested.

"Yeah. That was it. The idiot pretended he was Alex Cole, and the funny thing is that all three girls actually fell for it. At least, at first."

"What gave him away?"

"I'm guessing the premature ejaculation, the tears and then the threats," Don replied.

"Was there anything else?" Larry asked.

"There was some talk about some pets going missing in his neighbourhood. A couple of people swore they'd seen him burning some weird stuff in the backyard, but nothing ever came of it. Other than that, I can't think of a thing. As I said—the guy was a nobody."

21

CHAPTER

Aaron had to be up before sunrise. Toni was driving him to San Diego for his Comic-Con appearance. Diana arrived at the house at six-thirty so she could accompany them for the hundred and twenty-eight-mile journey. She had decided that as his panel discussion was at ten in the morning, they should make an early start and beat the inevitable gridlock of the Los Angeles morning traffic. Even on Saturday, the freeways could be snarled by eight.

This was the one event that Alex was sorry to miss. He loved the craziness of the conference and the passion of the people. He also realised that his being accepted by the Comic-Con fans as a bona fide sci-fi star was tenuous at best. When he had still been on the soap, he'd managed to score a small role in *Galaxy II, Neutral Conflict.* He only had five lines and was ultimately impaled by a rogue Cythian, yet his later success coupled with his brief appearance on the bridge of the Galaxy II somehow gave him enough G2 cred to warrant an annual invite to the convention.

Before Diana arrived, Alex had sat Aaron down and explained the importance of upholding his image in front of the conference crowd.

They were ardent fans, but at the same time, were highly critical of anyone they perceived as demeaning the Galaxy II brand or the Comic-Con traditions.

The drive took just over two hours. They pulled up at the Bay Front Hilton with enough time to grab breakfast and give Aaron a chance to freshen up before heading next door to the Convention Center.

The panel discussion started on time. The topic for the celebrity forum was whether computer effects were ruining some of the purity of sci-fi television and film. It was a hot topic. CGI could create almost anything the mind could imagine, which, for the world of sci-fi, gave the director an unlimited canvas. However, some purists, especially fans of the original Galaxy II TV series, missed the simplicity of the Styrofoam rocks and plastic disrupters.

The debate raged for the full hour and Aaron played his part well. Alex was a fan of modern effects and felt they gave the viewers the chance to experience other worlds and realities in a way that would have been unthinkable in the 1970s. Thankfully, Aaron shared Alex's opinion and was able to argue their case without any need for pretence.

Diana watched from her seat among the audience. She was surprised at how well Aaron was doing. The only slight hiccup came when the event was over and the panel guests stood to leave. Aaron made a beeline for Marta Sylvane, the Argentinian model and co-star of the *Dark Space* movies.

Diana couldn't hear what Aaron said to her, but she had no trouble seeing the actress's look of surprise and discomfort after he'd spoken to her. She also saw Aaron wink at her as he walked off stage.

"What did you say to Marta Sylvane?" Diana asked when she caught up with him.

"I just told her I was a big fan," he replied, feigning indignation.

"What else did you say?"

"Nothing!"

"I can always just ask her," Diana threatened.

Aaron rolled his eyes.

"Okay. I may have mentioned that her love scene in the zero-gravity swimming pool had made me so hot, I thought I was gonna come right there in the movie theatre."

"You said that to her?" Diana asked, shocked.

"Damn right," he replied. "She deserved to know how much I appreciated her work."

"Jesus," Diana shook her head. "You are one classy guy, aren't you?"

"I do my best," he grinned.

Twenty-five hundred miles away, Larry was just approaching the entrance to the Naples City Hall. The humidity was so bad that he'd worked up a good sweat just walking the two hundred yards from the visitors' parking lot to the front door. The place didn't look like anyone's idea of a government building. It looked more like a repurposed Howard Johnsons.

Jason had already greased the necessary wheel and the storage room was going to be 'inadvertently' left unlocked from 3:15 to 4:00 pm. All Larry had to do was walk in as if he belonged there, then rifle through some old filing cabinets. Or at least that had been the plan, as he'd imagined it.

He found storage room B at the very back of the building off a dank and abandoned-looking hallway. The door was unlocked as arranged, but when he turned on the overhead light, only one of the eight fluorescent bulbs came to life. Its ballast was buzzing, and the light flickered to the beat of some inaudible rhythm.

If there were filing cabinets in the room, they were buried under and behind the hundreds of file boxes that appeared to have been unceremoniously thrown in. Larry knew he only had forty-five minutes so opted for the reverse method of finding what he needed. Instead of finding Peterson's file, he first shifted any box that couldn't be of value. He knew that he needed to find a date range before 1998 which was when Peterson turned eighteen and ceased to be a minor in the state of Florida.

The loose boxes were all dated in the 2000s. Larry simply dumped them all off to one side and eventually uncovered the first filing cabinet. It took a further fifteen minutes until he found a grey, heavily scuffed metal cabinet that was starting to rust at the bottom. A yellowed label read 1985 to 1996. Aaron would have been five to sixteen.

Close enough.

Larry had planned on being discreet and leaving no trace of anyone having gone through the files, but with the state of the place and the clock ticking rapidly down to zero, he chose the bull-in-a-china-shop option. He tore at the drawers, found the Ps and saw four files for Peterson. All of them had the initial A.

Larry grabbed them and shoved them inside his sweat-dampened shirt. He gave the room a quick glance and wondered if anyone could possibly know that the place had been tampered with. He felt they couldn't. In fact, by unearthing the filing cabinets, he may have done the city a service.

He slipped out the back door which led to a baked sliver of bone-dry dirt, beyond which appeared to be an un-reclaimed section of the Everglades. Not being a fan of copperheads or gators, he stuck to the dirt track and eventually emerged about a half block down the street from the City Hall.

The second Larry was back in his rental car, he cranked up the air conditioning and placed the moist folders on the passenger seat with one vent pointing directly at them.

Back at the hotel, he opened the top file. The contents concerned a stabbing, but the A. Peterson was Andrew Peterson who was seventeen in 1986. The next one was for a black kid named Amos Peterson who had been accused of stealing fifty cents worth of chewing gum. The poor kid had been seven at the time yet some asshole, bigoted cop decided to put the little guy squarely into the system just for taking a stick of gum.

The last two Peterson files were about Aaron. One concerned the fire that consumed the family home and his parents. Fire investigators had found clear evidence of arson. Someone had poured aviation fuel around the entire perimeter of the house, then set it alight. Aaron had spent the night at a friend's and had thus been spared. As detectives started to peel back the layer of the onion, they found that though Aaron had spent the night at Jimmy Walsh's house, nobody at that house could guarantee that Aaron hadn't found a way to sneak back home and set the fire. In addition, the detectives found video footage of Aaron filling a portable gas can at Naples Airport less than a mile from his house. The date stamp showed the purchase to have occurred two days before the arson attack.

Aaron stuck to his story that the gas was for his Honda 50 motorbike. He swore that the Avgas made the old bike purr. When asked why he didn't just drive the bike to the airfield, Aaron claimed that someone had siphoned his tank the previous night, so he didn't have much choice but to walk. When they checked his bike, they found it was indeed filled with Avgas and when started, seemed to run surprisingly well.

Aaron was charged with two counts of premeditated murder but the District Attorney at the time looked at the minimal evidence and deemed it circumstantial at best. He was retiring in six months and didn't want to be remembered for putting a fifteen-year-old kid on trial with evidence that a first-year public defender could unravel before lunch.

He told the investigating officers the same thing he told the Chief of Police - "Get me some evidence I can run with, and I will." According to the file, they never did.

Larry opened the second Aaron file and saw that it was dated four years before the arson charge. Aaron and his best friend, a kid called David Finch, were standing at a bus stop on Tamiami Trail just before Bonita Beach Road. The driver of a city-contracted dump truck said that one of the kids, Aaron, pushed the other one right in front of his vehicle. His truck hit the kid, killing him instantly.

The responding officers arrested Aaron. Whether or not he did it became a moot point when it was discovered that the driver had both alcohol and cocaine in his system. Aaron denied pushing his friend and seemed distraught at his death. He swore that the driver swerved at David when he stepped off the curb so he could see if a bus was coming.

The charges were dropped, and the driver ended up losing his license, his wife, his job and seven years of freedom.

Larry put down the file and tried to will away the sense of foreboding he was starting to feel.

He reached for his phone.

Diana had forgotten to turn her phone back on after leaving the convention. She would normally have noticed when she called Alex to tell him how Aaron had performed. However, with Aaron sitting only inches from her in the back of the Range Rover, she could hardly phone or text without him knowing what was said.

Once back in LA, still unaware that her phone was off, she went straight home after Toni dropped her and Aaron at the Hollywood Hills house.

Larry tried Diana's phone three times without success. He didn't like going around her but felt that Alex and the others needed to know what he had found out about Aaron. He called his private cell and was relieved when Alex answered after the sixth ring.

"Alex, it's Larry," he began. "I'm calling from Naples, Florida. I can't reach Diana, so I thought it best that I speak with you directly."

"No problem," he replied.

"It seems that there is more to Aaron Peterson's background than we originally thought. I met with some people from SFI, and they pointed me towards some expunged police records as well as a couple of juvenile arrests. It's not good. I'm flying back to LA in about twenty minutes. It's just gone five o'clock here so I should be on the ground no later than seven-thirty your time. I want to swing by my condo for a few minutes then could meet you anywhere you want."

"Why don't you come up here at nine? I think we need to keep this private. I'll brief Diana but I think you should consider not discussing anything about this on the phone. You just never know."

"I agree," Larry replied. "I'll see you at nine."

"Have you seen my phone anywhere?" Alex called out from another room.

"It's in here," Aaron shouted back from Alex's study.

Alex walked into the room with a confused look on his face.

"This what you're looking for?" Aaron said pointing to the oversized iPhone 12 that he'd just placed on the desk.

"What are you doing in here?" Alex asked.

"I came in when I heard your phone ringing," he lied.

Aaron had managed to grab it when Alex was in the shower and couldn't hear his distinctive *Ride of the Valkyries* ring tone. He might have let it go to voicemail but seeing Larry Fritt's name appear on the screen was too tempting. Considering what he'd heard, he was damn glad he had answered it.

"I must be starting to lose it," Alex joked.

"You've got a lot on your mind. It's understandable."

Alex retrieved the phone then gave Aaron a pat on the back.

"I watched the stream from the Comic-Con forum," Alex advised.

"And?"

"You were amazing. I honestly don't think I could have done better."

"Thank you," Aaron replied with fake humility. "I had a good teacher."

"I may just let you be me forever," Alex joked. "I could use the break."

Alex again patted him on the back then left the room.

"Careful what you wish for, Alex," Aaron whispered to himself in perfect Alex Cole as he started to plan what he needed to do about Larry.

22

CHAPTER

Nobody in the house had any inkling that Aaron went out most nights. He'd found that by climbing over the guest house terrace railing, he could swing himself onto a small, levelled piece of hillside directly below the supporting wall. From there, it was a five-minute walk through some heavy brush, but after that, he would emerge onto an unpaved fire road that wound its way down to the back of the Chateau Marmont Hotel.

He kept his hoodie up and stayed away from people as best he could. He didn't want to be seen. He just sometimes needed to get away from the house. Leaving the property gave him a sense of freedom. He didn't feel like Aaron Peterson or Alex Cole as he moved within the shadows of the night. He was in between. He was a pupa hidden in the cocoon as it transformed from the insignificant caterpillar into the majestic butterfly. The metabolic and psychological process needed for him to fully become Alex Cole was not yet complete, but it would be soon.

Very soon.

Larry had taken a long shower. The sweat from the Florida humidity and the smell from the surrounding Everglades had hung on his clothes and body for over twenty-four hours. He was just putting on a clean T-shirt when his doorbell rang. Larry knew the building had a state-of-the-art security system on the front entrance and couldn't understand how anyone could get in without having to announce themself.

"Who is it?" Larry asked, keeping his door closed.

"It's me." The voice was muffled but still had the star's recognisable vocal lilt.

"Alex?" Larry asked.

"Who else would it be, my friend?"

Larry had no idea why Alex chose to reply in a bad Mexican accent, but he was, after all, an actor and therefore always 'on stage'.

Alex had never before come by Larry's Harper Avenue condo. It wasn't anywhere close to being the sort of home that Alex was used to, but Larry was proud of it. Three bedrooms, hardwood floors and only two minutes from Sunset. He'd furnished the 1930 unit with rich leathers and light woods. It was never going to make the cover of Architectural Digest, but it had been home to him ever since his wife had died and Larry had realised that their little house in Studio City held too many memories.

Larry opened the door, smiling.

"Come…," he started to say before realizing it wasn't Alex. "What are…"

The box cutter sliced through his throat before he had time to react.

"Oh, Larry," the voice whispered. "You should have let sleeping dogs lie."

Larry felt his legs give way under him. He tried to speak but produced nothing but blood bubbles from his open neck wound. He could see who he'd thought had been Alex looking down at him with what appeared to be compassion.

"It won't be long," the voice whispered. "Just let it take you. It'll be much easier than trying to fight it."

Larry tried to pull himself up with one hand while the other held onto his throat. His arm didn't seem to have any strength left in it. His vision started to blur at the same time as his body started to shiver. He fell back to the tiled floor.

Larry felt cold as the room seemed to go dark around him.

Then he felt nothing at all.

His visitor stared down at the unmoving body and growing pool of blood that was gathering within the floor's grout seams. The red fluid was expanding outward as it formed a strange, gory, geometric pattern between the tiles of the entry hall.

The killer sighed and tossed the boxcutter to the far side of the living room, before removing a zip-lock baggie from the hoodie. In it was a rumpled grey T-shirt and a second smaller baggie. After removing the T-shirt, then dabbing the garment into Larry's blood, it was carefully pushed back into the bag. After donning a pair of disposable shoe covers, the contents from the smaller baggie were scattered throughout the apartment.

Larry had converted the second bedroom into a home office. His laptop and iPad were both sitting on the desk.

That saved a lot of searching.

Toni drove Alex in the Range Rover while Aaron had to again have his hoodie up as Maria drove him in her car to Montecito. They left early to beat the traffic but ended up in a marine layer. It had stealthily managed to creep onshore, blanketing the 101 freeway with grey clouds, and, in some spots, dense fog. Much to Maria's surprise, Aaron was quite talkative. In fact, he seemed to be in an exceptionally good mood.

Once everyone arrived at the house and had done a little settling in, Maria whipped up a fresh fruit salad and croissants as a late breakfast. Aaron, Linda and Alex ate out on the back patio. Even the most intrusive paparazzi couldn't have photographed that part of the property.

"So, what does everyone have planned for this morning?" Alex asked. "How about watching the new Emma Tiel movie? It's supposed to be hysterical. The file came in yesterday so we can watch it in the theatre."

"I'm going to go for a walk in the hills. I need to get some air," Linda announced.

Alex gave her a strange look as she was, at that very moment, sitting out in the open air. He also noticed that she seemed to be glaring at Aaron when she spoke.

"That sounds nice. I might join you," Alex suggested.

"No, you stay here and enjoy your movie. I'd actually prefer to be alone if that's all right."

Before Alex could reply, Maria appeared.

"I'm sorry to disturb your breakfast but there are some people here to see you," she advised Alex.

"I'm not expecting anyone. What do they want?" he replied.

"I don't know, but…" Maria lowered her voice. "They say they're Los Angeles police detectives."

"Where are they now?" Alex asked.

"Still at the gate. I didn't know if I should let them up or not."

"Yes, of course you can. Let them in and I'll talk to them in my office."

"What do you think they want?" Linda asked as Maria scurried back into the house.

"I can't imagine. It must be important to drag them all the way up here," Alex commented. "Do you think I should call Freddie?"

"Who's Freddie?" Aaron asked.

"And tell him what?" Linda replied to Alex, ignoring Aaron's question. "If there is a need to involve a lawyer, you can always call him later."

Alex walked into his office and shook hands with the two detectives. Andrew Salk, grey-haired, fiftyish and still fighting to retain the youthful physique he had when he was in the Marines, spoke first.

"We'd like to question an employee of yours, one Antonio Gonzales. Normally, we wouldn't be asking permission, however, considering who…"

"Interviewing him about what?" Alex interrupted.

Detective Salk took a long deep breath. Dealing with celebrities was par for the course in Los Angeles, but when it involved something as serious as a murder, celebrities usually slowed the investigation down whether intentionally or not. In this case, it was twice as complicated. The victim appeared to have been doing some work for Alex Cole, or at least for his manager, who was still being questioned at her home in Thousand Oaks.

The other detective, Chris Baker, was black, fitter and seemed from his body language to outrank Salk, despite being ten years younger than the other detective.

"I believe you knew Lawrence Fritt. He was a contractor with Global Studios," Baker asked.

"Yes, but what do you mean *knew?* What's happened to him?"

"He was found late last night in his apartment in West Hollywood," Baker stated.

"He was murdered," Salk added.

Alex walked behind his desk and sat down heavily.

"I'm really sorry to hear that. We weren't exactly close, but he seemed like a good man. My manager, Diana Trent, was the one who dealt with him most of the time."

"We know. We spoke with Detective Morales earlier today. She filled us in on your relationship with the deceased," Salk replied.

"What's any of this got to do with Toni… Antonio?" Alex looked confused.

Salk looked to Baker for support.

"Mister Cole, at this moment, Antonio is a suspect in the death of Mr. Fritt. We only want to question him at this point, but depending on how he responds, it's possible that we will be forced to place him under arrest and take him back to West Hollywood for further questioning."

"But why?" Alex tried to keep the frustration from his voice. "Antonio had no reason to harm Larry. This is crazy. I'm going to call my lawyer now. Or maybe I should say, Antonio's lawyer."

"That's probably for the best." Baker nodded.

Alex called Freddie Rothstein on his private number. Alex was instructed by Freddie to put the phone on speaker, at which point Rothstein advised the two detectives that they were not to question his new client until he arrived, which would take about ninety minutes.

He then asked them a direct question.

"On what grounds are you basing your belief that Antonio Gonzales is in any way a suspect?" Freddie asked in a calm authoritative voice.

Baker stepped closer to the phone so as not to have to raise his voice.

"The murder weapon was found at the scene. It had multiple sets of prints on the handle…"

"Handle of what?" Freddie asked bluntly.

"It was a blue metal box cutter," Salk announced.

Baker shot him a glare. Salk knew better than to interrupt when he was on a roll.

"I assume you ran the prints?" Freddie asked.

"We did and they belonged to the suspect," Baker answered.

"What was used as the comparator?"

"He was arrested when he was nineteen for carjacking," Baker replied. "He was printed at the time of the arrest.

"Was he charged for that crime?"

"No. He was not."

"Is that it?" Freddie asked.

"No, actually there was a second set of prints on record," Baker announced almost proudly. "He was fingerprinted for a background check prior to being employed by Mr. Alex Cole."

"I see." Freddie sounded mildly disappointed. "Other than the box cutter, was there any other evidence that pointed specifically to my client?"

"A blood-soaked T-shirt was found in the building's communal dumpster. The blood type matches that of the victim."

"I assume that this shirt is tied to my client in some way?" the lawyer asked.

"Other than being on the premises and being covered in blood? Yes, there is something else," Baker stated flatly.

"Please enlighten me?" Freddie asked. The condescending tone was not lost on either detective.

"It was a large, dark-grey, Hanes cotton T-shirt..." Baker started to answer.

"That limits the subject pool to only a few million Los Angeles residents. I'm not sure I understand why you feel you can tie this garment to Mister Gonzales?"

Baker smiled. He had baited the pompous-sounding attorney perfectly. He rarely got to have what he considered to be fun in his job, but on the rare occasion when he could get one over on a defence lawyer, it made his day.

"Even if you found any DNA traces on the shirt, it will take days or even weeks to get the DNA compared to my client, so please tell me which forensic tool you used to determine the shirt's ownership?" Freddie asked, haughtily.

"It wasn't so much forensics as simple reading," Baker stated.

"I'm not sure I..." Freddie began.

"The T-shirt had a sewn-on label. Probably so that whoever did the washing wouldn't mix other people's clothes together. It was nicely done. It was printed instead of some quick job with a marker. Clear as anything. Black print on white cotton." Baker paused for effect.

"The label said... Antonio Gonzales."

23

CHAPTER

Baker notified Freddie and Alex that as Toni was now represented by an attorney and was therefore no longer going to willingly have an 'off the record' conversation with them, they had no choice but to charge him and take him into custody for the murder of Lawrence Fritt.

Baker advised that they were no longer there for a friendly chat and asked for Alex to tell them where to find Toni within the house. Alex knew that at mealtimes he would be helping Maria in the kitchen. He asked if he could escort the two men to soften the blow, but they advised that Alex was better off staying in his office.

The two detectives headed off to the kitchen with their right hands resting on their service weapons. Toni was putting plates into the dishwasher as the pair entered the room. Maria was removing a freshly baked apple tart from the oven and was startled to see the two men walk into her kitchen. They stepped quickly on either side of her husband. Salk roughly forced Toni's hands behind his back then handcuffed both wrists.

"Antonio Gonzales, we are arresting you for the murder of Lawrence Fritt," Baker stated. "You have the right to remain silent. Anything you say can be used against you in a court of law. You have the right to have a lawyer present during any questioning. If you cannot afford a lawyer, one will be appointed to you. Do you understand these rights?"

"I understand the rights. I just don't understand what I'm being accused of. I didn't kill anyone," Toni insisted.

Maria started approaching the officers and Toni.

"Ma'am, please stay where you are," Salk barked.

"This is my kitchen, and that is my husband," Maria shot back.

Baker removed his firearm and held it at his side.

"Ma'am, we are in the process of arresting this man. If you interfere, we will have no choice but to arrest you as well."

Maria looked to be about to continue her verbal exchange with the officers.

"That's enough!" Alex's voice echoed within the kitchen as he walked in.

"Officers, this is my home, and these are my employees. I understand that you have to take Antonio away until this can be sorted out, but you will not threaten anyone else in this house or I swear to God that I will see to it that neither of you ever hold a police badge again."

Salk looked about to argue the point, but Baker knew only too well that someone with Alex's connections could probably make good on the threat. It wasn't right and it wasn't fair, but it was the way it was. He gestured for Salk to not say anything else.

Both detectives marched Toni out of the house as Alex stayed behind to stop Maria from charging after them.

"This is supposed to be America. It feels more like my old home in Mexico where dirty policemen would drag you from your bed in the middle of the night."

"They're just doing their job. I have already got Toni the best lawyer in Los Angeles. He'll be fine, I promise."

"I would like to drive to Los Angeles so I can see him," Maria stated.

"That wouldn't be a good idea," Alex replied. "They won't let you see him, plus there is bound to be a great deal of publicity over this. You'll be hounded by photographers. Why not wait here until his lawyer gets Toni out on bail?"

"That's my husband they've taken away. I'm not going to stay up here in Montecito while he sits in some jail cell in Los Angeles. I'm going down there with or without your permission, but I strongly hope that you will honour my request."

"Maria, you're not a prisoner here," Alex insisted. "Of course, you can go. Just promise me that you'll stay in the house. You don't want to get yourself in any trouble at this point."

"Thank you, but I don't want to stay at your home," Maria said. "I will stay in our apartment in North Hollywood. It's not as close to the police station but I will be among friends."

"You're among friends here too, Maria," Alex reminded her.

She smiled and gave him a quick peck on the cheek.

"You are my employer, Mr. Cole, but thank you for saying that."

Her response drew blood. He knew she hadn't meant the statement to be harsh or critical, but it reminded him of the socio-economic distances between them that could never be fully bridged.

"I'll give Freddie all of your contact details so he can keep you up to date with what's happening. I'll also tell him that if any opportunity arises for you to be able to see Toni, he's to make sure that happens."

"Thank you," she answered. "The fridge is stocked so there's plenty to eat and the freezer's got lots of pre-cooked meals. At least you won't starve."

Alex watched her leave the room. He wished he could do more.

"What did the police want?" Linda asked as she carried some of the breakfast plates into the kitchen.

Alex explained the purpose of the visit and Maria's sudden departure.

"Have you called Freddie?" she asked.

"Yeah. He's going to meet them when they get to the West Hollywood police station."

"What are you going to do?"

"I'm just thankful that we're up here," he replied. "As soon as the media learns that Toni works for me and that Larry was doing some investigating for us, things are gonna go completely haywire. They'll try and turn it into some horrific conspiracy theory before Toni even gets bail. We are going to have to hunker down until this nonsense gets cleared up."

"Are you certain that Toni couldn't be involved in some way?"

"Of course, I am, aren't you?" he shot back. "You can't seriously think for a minute that Toni would have a reason, or for that matter, the means to kill Larry?"

"I suppose you're right, but…the shirt and the box cutter…that sounds awfully incriminating."

"What sounds incriminating?" Aaron asked cheerfully as he walked in with his empty plate.

"I wouldn't normally share anything this personal, but you'll end up hearing about it within a few hours anyway." Alex gestured towards the living room.

Once seated, Alex told him everything that he knew. He also stressed the importance of keeping an especially low profile on the property while the events ran their own course. If the media were to get even a whiff of a body double while they were already foaming at the mouth over a murder, the situation would instantly become untenable.

"That's cool," Aaron replied. "I get it. I'll keep my head down till you say it's safe."

"Is this a bad time for me to go for a walk?" Linda called out from the other room.

"Actually, it's probably the best time," Alex replied. "Once the media lays siege on our gates, none of us will be going anywhere."

"Mind if I join you?" Aaron asked. "Is that okay, Alex? I mean, it's probably the last daylight I'm gonna see for a while, right?"

"Sure, why not? We've got a few hours until we're under siege. Stay off the roads and stick to the trails behind the house. There's never anyone up there. And whatever you do, don't go near the front gate."

Alex didn't hear Linda curse under her breath from the other room. He was too busy answering his phone.

"Diana, thank God," Alex said. "I can't believe any of this."

Aaron slipped out of the room as Alex began pacing back and forth as he held his phone in a death grip against his ear.

"The important thing for you at this moment is to stay away from the press," Diana insisted. "That goes for Aaron as well. This thing has got too many moving parts. I don't like it when we can't control the narrative."

"I'm more concerned about Toni," Alex stated.

"I am too," Diana agreed. "But there's only two explanations that I can think of at the moment. Either Toni really did kill Larry and none of us knows the reason…"

"It's not that one," Alex interrupted.

"I don't think so either," she replied. "In that case, he's being framed by the actual killer. That worries me even more."

"Are you thinking it's the same person who shot me?" Alex asked.

"It's the only option that makes any sense. We know that Larry was still working with Detective Morales on trying to find the shooter. Maybe Larry had gotten a little too close."

"Could it have been something to do with his trip to Florida?" Alex suggested.

"That was unrelated. He was checking out some details about Aaron."

"What sort of details?" Alex asked.

"Apparently, he had some sort of juvie record plus a few arrests that ultimately never amounted to any formal charges."

"That doesn't sound that bad. I had a couple of arrests when I was young too," Alex commented.

"I remember. However, you were just acting out after your parent's death," Diana reminded him.

"Maybe Aaron was doing the same thing. He lost his folks not that long after I did."

"Good point. So, if it was the same person who shot you, how did he or she know that Larry was getting close?"

"I have no idea," Alex replied. "Have you spoken to Detective Morales about this?"

"Yes," she said. "All I seem to do at the moment is speak to the police."

"Why don't you come up here and hide out with us?" Alex suggested.

"I can't. I have to meet with the lead detectives at West Hollywood this afternoon and tomorrow, I'm opening up your house for the crime lab."

"Why would you do that?" Alex asked, astonished.

"I was served with a warrant this morning. Toni was living at your house at the time of the murder, so they need to search it. If I don't let them in, they will serve you and force you to come down to Los Angeles. I presumed you'd prefer the first option."

"You presumed correctly," Alex replied. "Maybe, after all of that's taken care of, you can sneak away."

"We'll see," Diana said. "You just take care of yourself. I don't like any of this."

"Ditto," Alex answered.

Aaron may have invited himself along for the walk, but Linda had no intention of talking with him or even being anywhere near him. She had kept ten paces ahead since they started up the higher trail. It was steep going and Aaron was having trouble keeping his breathing regular. He wasn't much of a walker and was especially unused to hill climbing, probably because southern Florida was as flat as a pancake.

They had hiked high above the residential streets and were halfway up a narrow unpaved fire trail, the sole purpose of which was to give fire-fighters some access to the densely forested hillside in the event of a fire.

"It's beautiful up here," he gasped.

Linda ignored him.

Aaron managed to find a burst of strength in his legs and caught up with her.

"I really am sorry about the other night. I was only joking."

"You had a fucking erection and were nuzzling my neck. How is that joking?" she demanded without even looking at him.

"I just wanted to see how far I could get with you while I was pretending to be Alex."

She abruptly stopped.

"So, how far would you have gone if I hadn't realised that you weren't Alex?" she asked.

"That's the thing. I knew you would catch on before anything happened," Aaron insisted.

"I don't believe you." Linda resumed her killer pace and made easy work of the steep incline.

Aaron was finding it almost impossible to keep up with her and speak at the same time. He just didn't have the lung capacity.

"What benefit could there have possibly been for me to have continued?" he wheezed. "If we had gone much further and you then found out it was me, I'd have been back in Florida that same night."

Linda ignored his bleating and strode up the dirt trail with a renewed vigour.

24

CHAPTER

Alex was staring out the living room window watching the marine layer as it slowly crept up the hillside towards his house. It looked like silky smoke as its tendrils slowly enveloped the surrounding homes and trees.

"Alex!" Aaron came stumbling into the room. "It's Linda. She's hurt."

"What do you mean, hurt? Where is she?" Alex tried to keep his voice calm.

"She fell. We'd reached the top of the hill and were walking along the upper trail when she tripped. She was a ways in front of me. When I got to her, she was out cold on the ground. I think she hit her head on a log by the side of the path. She was breathing but I didn't want to move her, and there was no phone signal or any people around that could help. I had to leave her there to get help."

"Calm down!" Alex grabbed his arm. "Can you accurately describe where she is?"

"Absolutely," Aaron vigorously nodded his head.

"Tell me exactly where you left her, and I'll relay that to the emergency responders. After that, you need to go to your room and lie low. There will be quite a few people up here soon and they can't see the two of us together."

"You're actually sending me to my room?" Aaron asked.

Alex gave him a cold stare as he called 911. Aaron shrugged and headed to the guest suite as instructed.

The first to arrive was an SBFD mobile search and rescue vehicle. The lead officer spoke to Alex in detail as another assembled a specialised drone on the hood of the city's Chevy pick-up.

Alex hated lying to the responders by telling them that he had been with Linda when she tripped and hit her head. He didn't feel that he had any other choice. If Aaron filled in for him at this point, Alex could see himself being excluded from the entire process of locating Linda and getting her to hospital.

The marine layer had reached Villa Miranda. The grounds of the property were morphing from being a greyed-out blur one moment to the usual sun-streaked estate the next. None of that seemed to faze the two officers.

Their drone lifted into the air during a momentary break in the fog then vanished into the mist seconds later. The pilot watched his iPad screen and was soon able to see the hills behind the house as the small craft rose above the low clouds.

Alex stood on the sidelines trying not to get involved and impede their progress. The lead officer was giving minute by minute updates to another rescue vehicle that was already nearing the start of the ridge trail.

"That's her, That's her!" Alex shouted as Linda's unmoving body appeared on the iPad screen.

Directions were passed to the other truck. Its driver announced that he was three minutes away. As they watched on the iPad, the truck came into view and pulled up next to Linda's body.

A man jumped out of the vehicle and ran to her side. Kneeling on the ground, he gave her a cursory examination.

"We're going to need air transport," his voice cracked over the radio. "There's visible head trauma and possible spinal injury."

The second man on the ridge called for the Search and Rescue chopper to airlift her out.

"This is Mobile-Air Echo Tango Seven. We're socked in. Suggest you try Los Angeles."

They decided that that would take way too long. A paramedic team that was waiting outside the gates for instructions joined the conversation. Though their vehicle couldn't make it up the fire trail, the rescue crew truck could. The paramedics grabbed everything they would need including a collapsible gurney and loaded it into the Chevy.

As they were about to climb in, Alex stepped forward.

"Is there any way that I could come with you? The woman up there is my girlfriend," he stated.

The lead officer was about to deny the request as there was only room for four in the crew cab but the officer who'd been piloting the drone spoke up.

"I'll stay here with the other vehicles. Mr. Cole can have my seat."

The lead officer seemed confused at his partner knowing the man's name, then it dawned on him who Alex was.

"Climb in and please don't get in our way," he gestured to the back of the cab.

The rescue vehicle sped through the gates and headed up into the hills. The remaining officer waited on the other side of the gates with the unmanned ambulance and other vehicles that had responded to the callout.

Aaron smiled from his vantage point, peering through the plantation shutters in the front room. He went to the bar and poured himself a large glass of Alex's best Scotch. He downed half the glass then looked around the room as if seeing it for the first time. He played the game he'd invented when they first flew him out from Florida. He called it *What If This Were Mine?*

The rules were simple. All Aaron had to do was take in his surroundings, then decide what he would keep and what he wouldn't once he became Alex Cole. In his mind, he could refurnish or entirely redecorate. When he was really in the zone, he could take it a step farther. Back in Los Angeles, he'd mentally knocked down the stupid apartment that had been built for the Mexican help. What a waste of prime real estate. He decided that he would build out a massive game room with a pool table at one end and a virtual reality gaming station at the other.

Aaron finished the drink and walked to the main hallway. He opened the outer door to the private theatre/man cave then stared for a moment at the daunting slab of steel that faced him. He reached into his pocket and retrieved his phone. He opened the notes app, and, reading the eight-digit number he'd saved after watching Alex open the door the first night he was there, entered it into the keypad.

The steel door slid back into the wall. Aaron walked down the stairs and surveyed the room. He checked every inch of every cabinet and drawer to make sure that there were no landline phones or anything else that could be used to fuck up his plan.

Aaron had a lot to do to get the space ready. He started making a list on a new notes page.

Water
Canned food
Can opener
Meds?
Booze?
Bedding
Check for landline phone.
Disable keypad.
Keep air on?

He couldn't think of anything else at that moment, but he was pretty sure that he had some time. Alex would almost certainly go directly to the hospital with Linda and might even stay the night there. No. On second thought, Aaron didn't think they'd let him do that. She'd be in the ICU, so he'd be banished to some waiting room and eventually get sent home.

That was if she didn't die. You never can tell with a head injury. She could wake up or just as easily start seizing and stroke out before they could do a thing. Then there was the spine injury the responder mentioned. Aaron had no idea what that was about. He presumed it could have been when her head and the log connected. Aaron surmised that it could have tweaked her spinal cord.

He wasn't a doctor and didn't know how all that stuff was connected. He certainly didn't understand how the hell she was still alive.

It was remarkable to Aaron how resilient the human body could be sometimes. After all, Linda was somehow still breathing yet he'd hit her hard enough with that fucking log to knock her head clean off. One thing he was certain of was that if she did come round, there was no way that she was going to be able to tell anyone what really happened. How she'd snubbed him one too many times and after the last one on the trail, he'd given her what his dad used to call 'one hell of a walloping.'

Yeah, he reflected. She wasn't gonna speak to anyone. Certainly not in a way that anyone normal would understand. When someone gets walloped that hard right in the brain box, things are going to get scrambled inside.

He'd never forget that sound.

There'd been a sharp crack at the same time as a hollow thud and a squelch.

Aaron started to giggle as he replayed in his head the assault on Linda.

"Did you get an ittle bump on the head?" he said in a baby-like voice. "Well, that's what happens when you're a bad little girl, isn't it?"

Aaron mimed swinging a baseball bat.

"And he scores!" he shouted, followed by an impression of a crowd's roar.

25

CHAPTER

Alex stood outside the doors to the ICU waiting for someone to tell him what was happening. The paramedics had given him a full account of what they were doing in the ambulance once Linda had been transferred from the rescue vehicle.

The flow of information ended the moment she was wheeled into the hospital. It wasn't as if he wanted special mollycoddling; he simply wanted to know how she was doing.

The paramedics had said that her pupils were responding to light which was a good thing, but her breathing was shallow, and her blood pressure was dangerously low. They staunched the bleeding and dressed the head wound but were most concerned about what was going on within her skull. Things like a subdural hematoma were not that uncommon with head injuries of that type.

"Alex Cole," a voice sounded just behind him. "Back with us again?"

Alex turned and saw the doctor who'd treated him after the boat accident.

"Doctor…Eisner, isn't it?" Alex asked, hoping he'd got the name right. "My girlfriend had a bad fall while hiking. She's in there."

Alex gestured to the closed doors of the intensive care unit.

"I'm sorry to hear that," Eisner answered. "I've literally just walked in. I had no idea."

"I've been standing out here for almost two hours and nobody will tell me how she's doing," Alex stated.

"Let me find out for you," Doctor Eisner said as he patted the other man's back.

Alex watched him disappear between the industrial grey swing doors. His mind flashed back to the night when his wife, Miranda, had been rushed to the same hospital after the cancer decided to give her one last slice of misery before finishing her off entirely.

Miranda had been in remission from leukaemia for almost three months and though shockingly frail, she'd managed to resume her daily walks and yoga. Colour had returned to her freckled cheeks, and she had even started to regain some of her appetite.

The biggest indication that she was getting better was when she announced that she was moving out of the guest room that had been equipped with a hospital bed and a bank of medical support equipment and was returning to the bedroom she shared with Alex.

Alex and Miranda spent their first night together in over a year. It had, at first, seemed strange and almost foreign to have someone sleeping next to him. The strangeness soon evaporated as the two fell asleep holding hands.

Two days later, Miranda woke in the middle of the night drenched in sweat and gasping for air. Paramedics had rushed her to hospital. She had contracted pneumonia. Miranda was immediately wheeled into the ICU and put on a ventilator.

Alex had been left standing in the hallway for what seemed like days, but what was probably just a few hours. A nurse had finally informed him that Miranda was sleeping and at that moment, was out of danger. Alex went home to grab a quick shower and a change of clothing. He also prepared a bag with Miranda's favourite things to have at her bedside.

He packed her dog-eared copy of Wuthering Heights, the photo of her and Alex taken on their honeymoon in Maui and her wristwatch that she hadn't been able to wear since the disease took away a third of her weight. He also included her greatest treasure, a four-leafed clover locked within a clear Lucite cube. The word IRELAND was etched on the side in swirling script.

She'd found it at the Fairfax swap meet while looking for quirky objets d'art. She had shown it to Alex who couldn't understand why she seemed so excited at such a cheap and obviously mass-produced piece of touristy merchandise.

"I can't explain it," she'd replied. "I just get the feeling that it's going to bring us lots of luck."

Alex had only taken a few steps back inside the hospital when the ER doctor had gently taken him aside. Miranda had died only minutes after Alex had left to go home. They had been trying to contact him, but his phone kept going to voicemail. He remembered switching it off while he'd been waiting outside the ER before leaving.

Ten days later, Alex, Codi and Diana had stood at the stern of LUCKY DANCER looking out over a grey, flat sea. There'd been no wind and a thin drizzle was fighting to take hold and grow into something more substantial.

Alex held out the special cremation urn that was 'guaranteed to decompose in water and was supposedly harmless to the sea life'. He looked to the others then gently placed it over the side. For a moment, it bobbed on the surface, then leaned to one side as seawater found its way through the gill-like vents at the top. It dipped below the surface as the three watched it sink until it joined with the deeper water and vanished from sight.

Alex then removed the Lucite cube from the tote he'd used to carry the urn. He stared at the bright green clover piece that seemed to float in the centre of it.

"Thanks for all the luck," Alex whispered before throwing the Irish novelty as far as he could.

It was a good, strong throw. It travelled in a long, curved arc before plunging into the bay over two hundred feet from the boat.

Alex sensed the ICU doors swinging open. Doctor Eisner approached him with a cautious smile.

"Is she okay?" he asked.

"They are going to put her into an induced coma so that the swelling in her brain has a chance to start healing," he announced. "They've also decided that if they see any signs of her condition deteriorating, she will be transported to Cedars Hospital in Los Angeles."

"What exactly is wrong with her?" Alex asked. "Why can't they treat her here?"

"They can, however, Cedars has one of the best head trauma facilities in the whole country. When she fell, her head struck the log here…"

Eisner pointed to a spot on his forehead just above the right eye.

"Her skull has a narrow fracture, but thankfully, the skull itself didn't shatter and splinter which could have sent bone fragments into the brain. The biggest worry is that there is a noticeable swelling at the front of the occipital lobe. That's the part of the brain that controls sight and the ability to determine colour."

"So, she could be blind?" Alex could hardly bear to even ask. Linda was an artist. Her eyes were everything.

"There's nothing to indicate that the injury has left her with diminished sight or any other sense," Eisner explained. "We won't know anything until the swelling has gone down and the bruising has had a chance to heal."

Alex nodded his understanding.

"Why not move her there now if Cedars is the place where she should be getting treatment?" Alex asked.

"She needs to be kept as still as possible for the time being. They'll move her if they have to, but only as a last resort."

"Is she going to live?" Alex asked bluntly.

"She's a strong healthy woman. It's always hard to know what will happen after a head injury, but, so long as she's a fighter, she'll be in with a good chance of recovery."

Doctor Eisner almost had to insist that Alex go home and get some rest. He told Alex that nothing was likely to happen in the next few hours and that the most important thing for Alex to do was to take care of himself and get out of the hospital. He stressed that at times like that, the patient was receiving all the care and attention while the significant other was left adrift and in the midst of mental anguish while surrounding themselves with feelings of despair and blame.

Doctor Eisner had no idea of the guilt that the other man carried within him over not having been there when Miranda had died. Eisner sensed Alex's inability to walk away from the hospital and had taken down his private cell number and promised Alex that he would call personally the very second that there was any change.

Alex had left his car at the house when he'd accompanied the paramedics. He ordered an Uber and was relieved to see that the one that had accepted the fare was less than a mile away.

As they approached the house, Alex noticed that the police had set up a mobile barrier keeping the crowd away from his gate. News vans, paparazzi and gawkers were held back as the driver edged past. Alex had completely forgotten about the murder investigation and the feeding frenzy that would incite.

At Alex's request, the driver dropped him at the main gate so that there was no chance of him seeing Aaron wandering around inside the house. As Alex approached the front door, he could hear music blaring from inside. He felt a momentary sense of anger at Aaron having taken such a liberty with his belongings, but then, in an unexpected wave of empathy, accepted that he might have done exactly the same thing in the other man's shoes.

Alex sometimes cranked the custom sound system when he was alone and feeling the need for a jolt of AC/DC or Rush. Aaron, however, had chosen hip hop. Alex could hear the pounding bass from the front yard. The sound system fed every room in the house and volume could be independently controlled, but to be able to hear it beyond his home's sturdy walls was a first.

He stepped into the house expecting to see Aaron in the front room where the main speakers were embedded in the wall. The room was empty. Alex turned the music down enough so that he could at least think. He read the song data on the iPad that controlled the Bang and Olufsen system. The artist was apparently called Babyface Ray. Alex had never heard of him, then again, he had never understood rap or hip hop. Alex felt so out of touch with the music scene that he doubted if he could name any hit in those genres for the past twenty years.

Alex wandered through the living room, the den, the kitchen, even his office. There was no trace of Aaron, yet the volume was set high in each room. As he headed down the main hallway, he saw that the outer door was open to the basement theatre. The steel security door was also fully retracted. The song's repetitive bass line came blasting up from the lower level. On top of that, Alex could hear someone below trying to play the drums in time with Babyface Ray's music.

Alex again felt anger rising up at the idea of the guy feeling empowered enough to play with his stuff. He realised that he was reacting in the same way as a small child would when someone took their favourite toy without asking and started to play with it. Alex took a long cleansing breath before stepping down into the basement. He told himself to chill. So what if Aaron's playing with your drums without asking? He's a guest, Alex reminded himself. After all, the poor guy was just letting off some steam. He was stuck alone in the house knowing that a murderer who was targeting Alex Cole had struck a second time. Alex put himself in Aaron's position. He would feel very alone and very vulnerable. Making as much noise as he could seemed as good a way as any for Aaron to keep the fear at bay.

Besides, it wasn't as if he was doing anyone any harm.

26

CHAPTER

It took Aaron a good few drumbeats before he realised that Alex was watching him from the bottom of the stairs. He grimaced guiltily, then used the Bluetooth remote to kill the music. The sudden silence was unnerving. It was as if the throbbing bassline had somehow found a way to sync up with Alex's heartbeat. He continued to feel the bass even after the music had stopped.

"I know I should have asked, but there was nobody here and I needed to get rid of some excess energy," Aaron announced as he stepped away from the kit. "How's Linda?"

"Not good. They've put her in a coma."

"Intentionally?" Aaron gasped. "They actually do that?"

"Apparently so," Alex replied. "They're keeping her that way while her body heals."

"Do they think she's gonna be alright or… well… you know what I mean?"

"I'm not sure I do, but at the moment it's too early to tell."

Aaron nodded his head in understanding.

"If you've finished down here," Alex said, "why don't we go upstairs and have a drink? I, for one, need something to calm my nerves."

"Oh my God," Aaron exclaimed. "It only just clicked. Your wife was in the same hospital, wasn't she? This whole thing has to be bringing back a whole truckload of shit for you."

"Nicely put," Alex sighed as he turned towards the stairs.

Something suddenly registered. There had been something wrong with the room. He always kept it free of clutter and yet he'd peripherally noticed that there were a couple of storage boxes as well as food and water piled against the wall at the far end of the room.

"What exactly are you doing down here?" Alex asked as he turned back to Aaron.

He never finished the turn.

His head exploded in pain as something struck him. There was a momentary flash of brilliant white light.

Then there was nothing.

Alex was in a fog. He couldn't see anything. There was a faint sound coming from what, to Alex, seemed to be a great distance away. He realised that he was hearing his own heartbeat. Alex sensed rather than saw another person close to him. He tried to open his eyes but even such a trivially simplistic action sent waves of nauseating pain through his body. He thought that, for the briefest moment, he could hear chewing, then the darkness descended upon him again.

"Come on, sleepyhead," a voice whispered from a million miles away.

Alex wanted to find his way to the sound, but everything was confused and dark. He thought he smelled potato chips but then that morphed into a different odour. He knew the smell but couldn't make his brain recall what it was. He tried to open his eyes but couldn't. He was so tired, but he knew he had to fight to get out of the dark world he'd fallen into. He tried again to lift his eyelids but felt himself slip back into the abyss.

Alex felt a sharp pain as someone slapped his face. He managed to open his eyes and saw himself standing looking down at him. He couldn't work out how he could be in two places at once, then, like someone lighting a match in a dark room, he could see everything.

"For a while there I thought I may have hit you too hard," Aaron stated. "That would have been a bitch. I don't want you dead yet. You're my insurance policy. You have to stay alive at least for a little while longer."

"I don't understand," Alex managed to say through dry chapped lips. "Why would you hit me at all?"

"Elementary, my dear friend. How else was I going to be able to restrain you?"

Alex hadn't even noticed that his wrists and ankles were bound together with cable ties.

"Aaron," Alex tried to sound authoritative. "Let me go right now and we'll find a way to work through this. If you don't, I'll…"

"You'll what? Squirm a little more? Piss yourself? Seriously…I want to know what you think you're going to do to me. In case you haven't noticed, I'm the one in control now."

"What do you want? Money?"

Aaron smiled down at him.

"I don't need anything else from you," he spat. "From now on, there's only going to be one Alex Cole. As of today, Aaron Peterson ceases to exist."

"What the hell are you talking about?" Alex said as he strained against the cable ties. "You can't fool everyone into thinking you're me. Someone's going to see that you're not. You can't honestly think that Linda is going to be fooled for a second?"

"I already fooled her for much longer than that. By the way, I liked the way it felt when she grabbed my cock. Anyway, it's not like she's even gonna know who she is, and that's if she survives at all. I'll give the bitch one thing; she's got a hard head. I swung that log like I was planning to hit a home run over the green monster at Fenway."

Alex actually flinched. He couldn't believe what he was hearing.

"She didn't fall?" Alex stammered.

"Wow," Aaron leered. "You catch on fast, don't you?"

"Why would you do that? She never did anything to you!" Alex shouted.

"First of all, that little slut had it coming. She treated me with disrespect from the moment I got here. But the main reason was just what you were saying. She could maybe tell the difference. I can't have people around me who can tell the difference. Then again, in her case, I don't think she would have minded the sort of difference I could show her."

Aaron grabbed his crotch and did a hip thrust towards Alex.

Alex simply stared at him with a look of confused disbelief.

"You're insane. It's not going to work. You haven't thought this through."

"Haven't thought it through!?" Aaron laughed. "It's all I've thought about since I was a kid. The first time I saw you on TV, I felt like I was watching my own future. I started teaching myself how to be you every minute of the day. I started living my life the way you were living yours. You were too busy becoming a big star to feel it, but we were connected. We were like twins, but even stronger.

Our lives were being played out in some sort of parallel time rift. Don't you get it? I was always you. Even when tragedy struck, it struck us both."

"If you're talking about Miranda…"

"Fuck Miranda. I was talking about your parents. Mommy and Daddy Cole. All burned up in that plane crash in Santa Monica. I felt your pain all the way in Florida, but it wasn't real. The pain wasn't mine. I had to find a way to have the same anguish so that I could continue to evolve in the same way as you."

A look of complete horror crossed Alex's face.

"You killed your own parents?" he asked in barely a whisper.

"Of course, I did," Aaron boasted and did a strange awkward pirouette in front of him. "It didn't have the class or the same epic visual as yours dying in a private jet as it exploded on landing, but I did the best I could. Mine still died in a fire, and just so I could make it as close as possible to your parent's death, guess what I used to start the fire? Seriously…guess!"

Aaron looked like a kid showing off some new trick to his family. His face looked strangely younger. The eyes, however, showed no trace of a child's innocence and excitement. They looked cold and lifeless.

"You give up?" Aaron giggled. "I used jet fuel! Yup, I used jet fuel just so they'd burn up the exact same way that your folks did. Isn't that cool?"

Alex realised at that moment that the man standing over him really was completely insane.

"I've got another secret," Aaron boasted. "Want to hear it?"

Alex just glared up at him.

Aaron got on his knees and leant his face against Alex's.

"I'm the ghost," he whispered. "I'm the shooter."

Alex pulled his head away in complete shock. Aaron got to his feet and did a strange little dance as he again giggled like a small child.

"You said that I didn't think this through, didn't you?" Aaron preened. "What do you think now? That enough planning for ya, big guy? So, please… no more telling me how this isn't going to work. It's already working, and so far, I like the way it's going. There is only one thing I have to do to make the whole thing perfect. Can you guess what that is?"

The creepy child look was back, only this time Aaron's dead eyes seemed to sparkle.

"I have to finally unite with the woman who was always meant to be mine."

Alex pulled at the restraints with all his strength.

"You've worked that part out, haven't you, Alex?" Aaron crooned. "It's time for Alex Cole and Cindy Snow to become one… if you know what I mean. You do know what I mean, don't you, Alex? I'm going to do what you should have done over twenty years ago."

"You're a monster," Alex seethed.

"Am I, Alex? I like to think of myself more as someone who will do anything to get what he wants. If that's monstrous, then there's a whole lot of us out there." Aaron grinned. "Anyway, I'm going to have to leave you now, but there's food, water and bedding at the back of the theatre. I know that this room has its own air supply and you'll be happy to know that I've left that running. I need you to stay alive for just a little bit longer."

"Why?" Alex said through gritted teeth.

"As I said, you're my insurance policy. I've got some chores to do over the next few days. You know…getting rid of the dead wood, so to speak. The difference this time is that if something goes wrong and there's no way for me to continue being Alex Cole, I'm just going to anonymously tip off the cops that the murderer is in this basement, then I'll slip away and resume my boring life in Florida."

"Nobody's going to think that I'm you. That I'm the one responsible for all of this," Alex stated.

"Maybe not immediately, but as more people surface who say they saw you near Diana Trent's house, or near Codi Walsh's compound in Bel Air, people will start to doubt you. Then there's that little lie you told about being with Linda when she tripped. Once they check out that log and find some of your DNA and hair on it, I doubt they're going to buy your story about a twin you hired to pretend to be you. We took extra care to make sure that nobody ever saw the two of us together, didn't we? And as for the few that do know about me… well, they might just not get to stay alive for that much longer."

"It won't work. You can't just keep killing people. Why don't you go back to Florida now and I won't tell anyone about what you've done?"

"Seriously?" Aaron asked. "You'd do that for me?"

"Of course, I…"

Aaron sucker-punched him on the jaw, knocking Alex out cold.

"Alex, Alex, Alex," he cooed. "When are you going to stop treating me like an idiot?"

Aaron retrieved a folding hunting knife from his pocket then walked over to the base of the stairs and used the blade tip to remove the four screws that were holding the room's Crestron control unit to the wall. He yanked it roughly towards him, severing the dozens of cables that ran into the wall. Aaron took one last look around the room then ran up the stairs two steps at a time. He entered the code into the working controller in the hallway and activated the door lock. He was about to walk away when something struck him.

He found a flaw in his plan.

The idea of having Alex around to take the blame if things went bad was pure genius. That he knew. But he realised that there was actually no reason to keep him alive. A dead Alex wouldn't even be able to deny the charges.

He slapped himself hard across the face.

"Idiot!" he screamed. "If you want to be in charge, then you'd better be the smartest person in the room."

Aaron's impression of his father's attempt at mentoring him was flawless. For a moment, Aaron was saddened that nobody was around to appreciate it.

He turned back to the controller and brought up the master menu. He pressed the tab which read AIR SUPPLY/FILTRATION then pressed the red OFF tab. Aaron knew it would be quicker to just go back down and finish Alex off then and there, but he wasn't sure whether he could. They'd basically become the same person and just like the cyborg in the movie *Terminator* who was programmed not to kill the good guys, Aaron didn't know if he could even carry out the assassination of himself.

Aaron wanted to try one more failsafe measure and change the master code for the controller—the one that would let someone with the code override everything. He tried to use the password that he had but a message kept coming up saying that he was user number 1 and that if access to the administrator functions was required, to please enter the administrator code.

Aaron wanted nothing more than to rip the unit from the wall but had no idea if that would, in fact, trip some emergency door opening or some other function that could end up biting him in the ass.

He breathed away the anger. It wasn't easy, but Aaron found that by imagining Cindy waiting for him in LA, he was able to push the fury down into the dark place. It wouldn't actually abate down there, but it could at least lie dormant while he finished the last few chores before he finally became Alex Cole.

27

CHAPTER

Aaron walked up the curved stairway leading from the main entry hall and found the room he was looking for. He stepped into Alex's bedroom with a feeling of awe. He was no longer walking in as the upstart mimic. This was now his room. He placed the bottle of gin he'd been swigging from onto a mango-wood side table then opened a pair of ebony closet doors.

Lights faded up to the perfect luminance for dressing and admiring oneself. The walls were lined with rich handcrafted shelves, drawers and hanging spaces. In the centre of the room was a black, studded leather bench. At the far end was a three-sided space lined with floor to ceiling mirrors.

Aaron started with the shirts. He noted that Alex wasn't into bright colours. There had to be twenty shirts just in the white range. There was a dozen or so in the creams, then another twenty or so in the earth tone realm. All of them were expensive and elegantly tailored. Below the shirts were several drawers filled with T-shirts.

Aaron was relieved that these at least came in an array of colours. There were no 'in your face' primaries like the reds or blues that he would have worn. Instead, the colours, though varied, were softly muted and mainly in shades of pastel. Another set of drawers held polo shirts. The palette was the same. Aaron was disappointed to see that none of the shirts seemed to have any visible logos or branding.

He shook his head. He couldn't fathom why anyone would pay a fortune for clothes that didn't display a logo that showed everyone who you were wearing. Aaron always felt better when he wore one of the discounted Ralph Lauren shirts he bought at Marshalls or Ross.

Aaron spent over an hour in Alex's dressing room. Once he'd gotten a good feel for the whole inventory, he laid out the outfit he was going to wear for his big night.

He wanted to impress Cindy but didn't want to look as if he was trying too hard. He chose a pair of beige linen trousers with a pale aubergine-coloured polo shirt. Picking the right pair of shoes was more difficult. He really didn't like Alex's taste in footwear.

Whereas Aaron lived in New Balance all terrains, Alex seemed to favour narrow, Italian slip-ons. The biggest problem was that all the shoes were a couple of sizes too large for him. He had assumed that the fancy clothes they had given him to wear all came right out of Alex's closet.

The shoes sure as hell didn't. Aaron debated wearing one of the pairs they'd bought him so he could look like Alex, but they were too boring. He'd already found what he wanted to wear. It was a pair of pale dusty-blue casuals made by someone called Stefano Ricci. Aaron caressed the soft leather and knew that they were what was needed for a special night with Cindy.

He tried them on and saw immediately that his feet were too small. Aaron didn't care. He loved the look. He ended up wearing three socks and wedging a fourth at the toe end of each shoe.

They were uncomfortable as hell, but, as he twirled in front of the three mirrors, he didn't care. He began dancing to a Latin beat that was playing in his head. He felt alive and empowered. In his carefully chosen outfit, he knew he looked like a star. Not just a modern-day version, rather, he felt that he was more like one of the old classic stars; Cary Grant, maybe, or Gene Kelly.

He stopped moving and walked up to one of the mirrors.

"I'm Alex Cole," he said in a low gravelly whisper. "I've been waiting a long time to tell you this, but I think I love you."

Aaron moved closer, and, while keeping his eyes riveted on those within the reflection, he kissed the mirror.

He felt the erection growing in his new silk underwear.

He caressed it through his clothing while still kissing his reflection.

He unzipped himself and let the trousers fall to the floor. He pulled his penis through the opening in the briefs and began to stroke himself. The kissing became more passionate. More desperate. After only a few seconds, he came, sending a stream of opaque jizz onto the mirror.

A phone began ringing.

Aaron lifted the trousers up around his waist and stumbled over to the leather bench. He found his jeans under a pile of clothes and located the cell phone that he had taken from Alex earlier that evening.

"What?" he shouted angrily.

"Alex? Is that you?" Diana asked, sounding concerned.

"Sorry," he replied in a calm Alex voice. "I was trying to make dinner and just dropped an egg on the floor."

"That's because you don't cook. How's Linda?" she asked.

"She's in hospital. She fell while she was hiking in the hills."

"Is she alright?" Diana sounded concerned. "I heard something on the news."

"She's fine," Aaron lied. They're just keeping her in overnight for observation."

"That's a relief. I'm surprised you're not staying there with her," Diana replied.

"How do you know I'm not?" he fired back.

"I don't think they'd let you try to cook eggs in the hospital, do you?"

Aaron forced a relaxed-sounding laugh, though inside, he was furious at himself for getting caught out so easily.

"They sent me home. Said I was in the way."

"I've certainly felt that way about you a few times," she joked.

Aaron forced another fake laugh.

"Anyway, the reason I called was that the police have accessed Larry's email account and found an updated copy of the background check on Aaron Peterson."

Aaron felt his insides go cold.

"That must be a boring read," he responded.

"Actually, it's not. Larry must have finished it on the plane. It seems that Aaron may not be the most stable person in the world. I'm going to send you a copy right away and let you be the judge, but I think that we may have to cut the guy loose."

"You mean fire him?" Aaron tried to sound surprised.

"You read it and let me know what you think," Diana suggested. "Meanwhile, lock your bedroom door tonight."

"Will do," Aaron laughed as he disconnected the call.

He stood staring at the phone in his hand then suddenly screamed maniacally at the top of his voice and hurled it at the mirrored enclosure.

The iPhone hit the middle mirror dead centre.

It exploded into a thousand silvery pieces that rained down onto the cream-coloured Berber carpet.

Diana placed her phone back onto her coffee table.

She was worried. Alex sounded off. Then again, she reminded herself, Linda was in hospital. That would be enough to send him a little wacky.

"Shit!" she exclaimed.

It dawned on her that it had to be the same hospital where Miranda had died.

She reached for her phone and called him back.

It rang six times then went to voicemail.

"I realised that I wasn't being much of a friend. I just put two and two together. You mustn't think that what happened to Miranda is going to happen to Linda. She's strong, healthy and just bumped her head. Anyway, sorry if I sounded abrupt before. Call me whenever."

Aaron had known from the first moment he met Diana that the little bitch had to die. All that self-important attitude of hers got right under his skin. Why the hell Alex would let someone like her run his life, he had no idea, but one thing was now very clear - as soon as he'd crossed Cindy off his list, he would have to start planning a little surprise visit to Thousand Oaks.

He closed his eyes for a moment and visualised Diana opening her front door and smiling as she saw who was standing in front of her, the smile suddenly vanishing from her nasty little lips as Aaron slid one of Alex's expensive carving knives between her ribs.

Aaron had to smile. Just the momentary fantasy had been enough to engorge his cock all over again.

"Down, boy," he whispered to his erection. "Save yourself for later."

28

CHAPTER

Besides his phone, Aaron had also lifted Alex's keys from him when he was out cold. He hoped that one of them would fit the mystery garage. He really didn't want to have to drive the giant Range Rover all the way to LA. He was in the mood to drive something a little classier.

The fifth key slid into the lock. A beeping sound erupted immediately from a control panel inset into the wall to the right of the door. Aaron hoped that Alex had used the same security code as he had inside the house, or else he was royally screwed. It turned out it was the same code, and the panel lights went back to green.

He flipped on the lights and gasped out loud. Considering Alex's wealth, Aaron had thought him to be something of a vanilla kind of guy. His houses were nice but not befitting someone who earned thirty million dollars a picture. The boat was okay but even a successful dentist could afford the payments on one like it. As for his cars... Aaron had assumed he would have no imagination whatsoever.

Not anymore.

There were five vehicles in the mystery building, one behind each garage door like a game show giveaway, though Aaron had ever heard of any show that gave away cars like the ones he was looking at.

Being raised in Florida, especially in a 'show it if you got it' kind of town like Naples, had given Aaron an early appreciation of fine cars. Porsches, Mercedes and Beamers were so common in Naples that the help drove them. Even the entry-level Ferrari, Maserati and Lambo didn't turn heads as they cruised down 5th Avenue towards the Gulf.

What was in Alex's garage weren't the most expensive cars by a long shot, neither were they the newest. They were, however, iconic examples of cars from a different era. Aaron couldn't see a theme that might have tied them together, but assumed that each one must have held some particular fascination or memory for Alex. He somehow knew that they hadn't been bought for investment or one-upmanship. These were obviously cars that he loved.

At the far end of the garage was a bright orange 1970's Ford Mustang, Mach 1. Next to that was a 1980's series white Porsche 911 turbo. The next one was a beige 1970's convertible Rolls Royce Corniche. An immaculate convertible Chevy Stingray was next, but the one that Aaron couldn't stop staring at was a dark blue 1980's Aston Martin Vantage.

It was gorgeous.

He decided that if he was going to really impress Cindy, pulling up in that set of wheels would probably do the trick very nicely.

It started on the first try. Thankfully, a garage door remote was clipped to the driver's visor. Once the door was fully retracted, Aaron revved the V8 a couple of times within the garage so that he could enjoy the throaty echo.

He drove to the front of the house and down the drive. He was amazed to see that even at that late hour, there were still some TV vans and paparazzi clustered around the front gate. Aaron gave them all a big wave from behind the Vantage's tinted windows as he turned out of his property. Once past the human detritus, he pointed the car towards the foothills and the 101 freeway.

Aaron stayed on San Ysidro Rd and cruised through the small downtown area of Montecito. The quaint Mediterranean-style shopping area was busy with the wealthy foraging for cashmere and designer handbags. Though it wasn't yet dark, dusk was only a short time away from beginning its nightly performance. The wrought iron streetlights were on early and though not yet producing much in the way of illumination, they gave the place a feeling of peace and wealth.

Aaron had always wanted to be rich. He wanted to be able to stare down upon the lesser people the way he would sometimes watch ants toiling away at meaningless repetitive chores. Whenever he could get away from school or his parents, he used to walk up and down 5th Avenue in Naples and pretend to window shop outside the expensive stores and galleries.

He wasn't shopping at all.

He was watching and observing how the rich behaved; how, when car doors were opened for them by valets or their own drivers, they never once made eye contact with such lowlifes. It was as if they were scared just in case the simple act of looking directly into a working-class retina could somehow pass along the DNA of poverty.

Even at seven years old, which was when he first started training to be rich, Aaron was able to mimic their walk and attitude. He learned to always keep his head held high and to never look down. Looking down only revealed dirt and scum. The trick was to look no lower than shoulder height.

As Aaron got older, he would sit outside the cafés and restaurants (eating or drinking the cheapest thing on the menu) and eavesdrop on their conversations.

The wealthy did not talk about petty nonsense like car repairs and grocery shopping. You'd never hear them questioning whether there were enough coloureds to warrant doing a cold wash in the clapped-out Maytag on the service porch.

They talked of future plans to meet up in Cannes or perhaps nip over to Nassau for the weekend. Though their very existences revolved around money, Aaron never once heard it come up as a subject for discussion.

By the time he reached his early teens, Aaron despised the lower classes. The fact that he lived on the wrong side of the Naples tracks seemed lost on him. The more time he spent around the Naples elite, the more it sickened him to have to sit in the overheated schoolrooms at Collier County High. He came to detest having to be surrounded by the spawn of plumbers, boat repairmen and roofers.

It wasn't until he was fifteen, when one of the older girls at school walked right up to him and kissed him on the mouth, that his life began to have direction.

The girl had been standing with her vapid friends by their lockers, discussing how much Aaron looked like the actor on the new soap, Days and Nights. Apparently, Alex Cole was, after only a few weeks on TV, already becoming something of a heartthrob. Her friends had dared her to kiss Aaron as it was about as close to kissing the real thing as any of them were likely to get.

When she returned to her group, they all asked what it was like.

"His skin's kinda oily and he has really bad breath."

They all howled as they walked by a confused and frustrated Aaron.

"What did I do?" he shouted after them.

"You look like Alex Cole," one of them called back.

It took Aaron over a week of glancing through supermarket fan magazines until he finally saw his first picture of Alex. He could still remember the shiver that had travelled the whole way up his spine as he stood alone at the check-out counter.

He did look like Alex Cole.

It wasn't until he had surreptitiously recorded an episode of Days and Nights *on his dad's VCR that his infatuation started to form.*

The plan to steal Alex Cole's life came much later.

After driving up the steep grade from Camarillo, Aaron saw the various exit signs for Thousand Oaks. He realised that he was within spitting distance of Diana Trent's house. It hadn't been part of that night's plan, but what, he wondered, was stopping him from having some fun with Cindy, then swinging by Diana's for a little dessert on the way home?

Maybe he'd pick up something sweet from the supermarket hardware aisle.

Perhaps a hammer would be the most fun. See how long that little uptight bitch could keep up that superior attitude while he bashed a little sense into her.

As if feeling Aaron's proximity, Diana Trent sat up straight on the couch and turned off the sound on her TV. She'd been having a funny sensation all night. Something had been bothering her. She felt that there was a thought or idea stuck somewhere in her brain that she couldn't seem to shake loose. It was like having an itch, but not being able to find where to scratch.

She'd been fidgety and unable to get comfortable since she'd spoken to Alex. No matter what she did, the sensation was still there.

"Shit," she exclaimed as she pushed herself up from the couch.

She knew that just sitting there wasn't going to squeeze the missing thought nugget from the dark part of her mind. She knew herself well enough to know that whenever a name or idea was lost in a cobwebbed corner, the only way to shake it loose was to focus on something completely unrelated.

She made herself a cup of camomile tea, switched the TV sound back on and pressed the GUIDE button on the remote. The Spectrum Cable guide appeared instantly. Though she forked out a small fortune every month to access every premium movie channel they had, she still liked to see what was on the more obscure, syndicated channels.

She scrolled through the selection until she came to WPFT which was showing one of Alex's worst movies. *Second Time of Life* had been a concept film marrying a typical buddy-style action flick with a reincarnation theme. The script itself had read well but the movie had received a thumbs down from both Roger Ebert and his guest co-host who was filling in for the ailing Gene Siskel.

Diana decided that it was perhaps the best distraction she was going to find.

The movie had been playing for half an hour. Diana watched as Alex and Peter Fein, another up and coming actor at the time, were forced to join a wet T-shirt contest on a beach where they were trying to observe a possible killer; their killer, in fact.

Diana shook her head at the appalling direction. Then suddenly, she paused the film.

The coin had finally dropped.

It was the phone call she'd had with Alex earlier in the evening. The weird feeling of discombobulation had started right after that.

She replayed the call in her head. He'd sounded a little stressed over the broken egg but otherwise, he been fine.

Then it hit her. The egg. He'd been making eggs for dinner. Alex hated the entire concept of breakfast for dinner or lunch or any other time that wasn't first thing in the morning. It was like a real thing with him. He would go off on a jag about how people would next be eating roast turkey with all the trimmings at six in the morning.

It felt as if a Klieg light had suddenly gone on in her head.

She started to recall funny little oddities in his phrasing and cadence.

She then knew what was wrong.

She hadn't been speaking with Alex at all.

29

CHAPTER

Once passed Woodland Hills, Aaron grabbed Alex's damaged cell from the centre console. The screen was cracked but thankfully, the device still worked. He selected Cindy's home number. It rang eight times then went to voicemail. He tried again.

Cindy answered on the fourth ring.

"This had better be good," she barked. "I was just getting into the bath."

"Without me?" Aaron asked in what he thought was a seductively witty voice.

"What the hell does that mean?" she barked back. "Do you know what time it is?"

"I… ugh… nothing. Look, I need to see you. It's got to be tonight."

"What do you mean you need to see me tonight? You're not coming over here this late."

"I don't want to say anything over the phone," Aaron said, "but I have to see you right now. There's things that have to be said."

"Is this about Linda?" Cindy asked, suddenly sounding worried. "I heard about the accident on the news. Please tell me she's alright?"

"She's fine. This is about you and me."

"Have you been drinking?" Cindy asked.

"Of course not," he lied. "I just wanted to let you know that I am coming by. See you in a few minutes."

"No," Cindy said emphatically. "If it's that important then fine, but give me at least an hour."

She disconnected the call.

Aaron could picture her in a white terrycloth robe, standing waiting by a sunken jacuzzi tub. The wind was blowing causing the robe to part revealing her nakedness beneath it. Her hair was billowing to one side and was lit from the overhead lights. It looked like spun gold.

A deafening horn shattered the image. It took him a second to realise that he'd drifted out of his lane and had been about to veer in front of an eighteen-wheel big rig. Shaken, he pulled back into his lane then saw that he had missed the three-lane merge with the 405 heading south.

Aaron decided that missing the turn may have actually been a good thing considering he now had an hour before seeing Cindy. He stayed on the 101, turned off on Woodman then made his way to Ventura Boulevard. He had come up with the perfect way to kill some time.

Considering that he was about to finally consummate his relationship with Cindy and had only just taken on the full Alex Cole identity, it was blatantly obvious that a celebration was in order.

He drove along Ventura, trying to find the perfect place to formally launch the new and improved Alex. A retro, green neon sign rose twenty feet into the air from the front of a drab 1950 stucco building.

It pulsated with the word, 'CURVES'.

He could see a crowd of people gathered inside. Aaron pulled the Aston Martin up in front of the bar and watched as a lethargic-looking valet-parking attendant opened his door.

Aaron took his time getting out of the car. He wanted his first entrance to be perfect. He knew the valet would fawn over him the moment he saw who had just alighted from the vehicle.

The man never even looked him directly in the face. He simply handed Aaron a parking stub, slid into the car and drove away.

Aaron walked into the bar and was stunned at how crowded it was. From the outside, it had appeared comfortably busy. Inside, it was like a mosh pit. He had to squirm and contort himself through the crowd to reach the bar which ran the entire length of the room. It was made from some sort of clear Lucite-like material that had been filled with thousands of flickering LED lights. They were blinking and drifting through the entire colour spectrum in time with the music that was being played at a painful volume.

It took him three attempts to get the attention of one of the bartenders. There were four of them and they were all extraordinarily curvaceous women. The one who eventually acknowledged him was tall, black and bald. She was also stunning. Aaron was momentarily tongue-tied.

"Better speak up," she said. "If you're not ready, I'll come back later."

"No… I'll have a gin and tonic," Aaron managed to announce. "Hendricks if you have it." Aaron knew that it was Alex's favourite.

The drink arrived and he downed half of it before the bartender asked if he wanted to run a tab.

He did.

Aaron turned away from the bar to survey the masses. He was amazed that nobody had, as yet, recognised him, or if they had, they were playing it very cool. He saw a cute redhead jammed amidst a group of friends. He gave her his best Alex Cole crooked smile.

She smiled back and laughed. Alex was about to move closer to her when he saw the woman whisper into a man's ear. He turned and faced Aaron. He was smiling, but it seemed to not be one of amusement. It looked more like a grimace.

The man broke from his peers and fought his way over to Aaron. As he approached, Aaron could see that the guy was big. Not just tall. He was big all round and none of it looked like fat. His hair was cut super-short, and he had a full beard that didn't look as if it got too much grooming.

"You're him, aren't you?" the man asked.

"If you mean, am I Alex Cole, then yes," Aaron replied with a cocky swagger.

"I've seen your movies," the guy stated.

"Most people have," Aaron replied.

"Why don't you come over and have a drink with us?" the man asked.

Aaron agreed and spent the next half hour pretending to be impressed as the men talked about sports fishing and the woman talked about Guy North, a new, much younger action film star who was making quite a name for himself.

"You know, I do most of my own stunts," Aaron suddenly announced, needing to rake in a little attention.

"That must be dangerous," replied the redhead he'd spotted from the bar.

"It is, but I feel it gives my characters a sense of realism," Aaron said, having to shout to be heard.

"Maybe one day you could take me on the set with you?" she said, swishing her red hair from her right shoulder to her left.

"I don't see why not," Aaron replied giving her a flash of Alex's trademark lopsided grin.

"You play a tough guy," her bearded boyfriend stated as he stepped between them.

Aaron didn't know how to respond to that, so he shrugged and laughed.

The man punched him once, fast and hard in the solar plexus. Aaron doubled over. The man bent down and whispered in his ear.

"I just wanted to check how tough you really were. Now I know."

The man walked back into the sea of people. It took Aaron a good few seconds to be able to breathe freely. He was still doubled over and was astounded that nobody bothered to see if he was okay. He couldn't even see the group he'd been drinking with. In pain and embarrassed, Aaron started for the front door. A cute waitress in a black leather jumpsuit blocked his way and handed him his bar tab. He was stunned to see that it was for over $800 dollars. Clearly, his new friends had been charging all the drinks to him. Aaron was momentarily terrified by the huge number until he remembered that he had Alex's wallet in his pocket.

"Want to settle up?" she asked.

Alex opened his eyes and saw that he was alone in the basement theatre. His jaw was sore from the sucker punch, but as he opened and closed it, he could tell nothing was broken. When he tried to move, he realised that his ankles and wrists were still bound together with cable ties.

Alex wasn't the most practical individual but was, however, inexplicable adept in the use of the cheap plastic fasteners. He used them to fix just about anything that ever needed binding. He also knew that the regular consumer variety were unsuitable as human restraints. He'd once tried on a pair of police issue ties at a charity gala and had been amazed at how strong they were. The ones that Aaron had used, presumably pilfered from the toolbox in the utility room, were relatively easy to defeat.

Alex went to work biting down on the fragile plastic ridges along the loose end of the cable tie. After he'd managed to flatten the ratchet-like bumps, he was able to force the plastic locking section onto the chewed area. It certainly wasn't helping his aching jaw, but he freed his hands in less than five minutes.

The ankle restraint was much harder. Unable to contort himself sufficiently to chew his way to freedom, he ended up using the metal tongue from his belt to pry apart the plastic locking block on the cable tie.

Alex got to his feet and surveyed the room. The first thing he saw was that the basement control unit had been ripped from the wall. When he'd had the room built, they'd planned for the possibility of getting accidentally locked in and had Crestron fit a landline phone connection into the control panel. With that having been destroyed, there was no way to call out of the theatre.

He made his way over to the pile of stuff that Aaron had left there for him. There was some clothing and canned food. There was also enough water to last him a month. He saw a toothbrush and toothpaste, which was a nice touch, but with no toilet or sink in the room, Alex decided that any such grooming could get messy real fast.

Alex walked around the entire circumference of the space examining it in a whole new light. When he'd designed it and had it built, his focus had been on how to make people want to be in it. Now, he needed to find a way to get out of it. After only one circuit of the room, he felt hot and slightly breathless. He initially put that down to the blow he'd taken to the back of the head, but then a horrible thought occurred to him.

He walked back to the south wall and looked up at the six-foot brushed chrome vent mounted a few inches below the ceiling. There was no sound in the theatre. It had been designed that way. Alex had wanted nothing to interfere with the audio quality coming from his professional cinema sound system.

One of the hardest things they'd had to mitigate in the enclosed room was the noise that came from the independent Oxyflow system that provided a constant flow of breathable fresh air into the room. The handler itself was outside but the sound of air travelling through the aluminium ducting was still audible. They'd had to create curved ducts to finally stop the noise.

At that moment, Alex wanted to hear the sound of air rushing into the room. It was the only way for him to know whether the system was in fact on. Alex knew that it had better be, as the room had been built hermetically sealed. Without the Oxyflow system, no trace of outside air could ever find its way into the room.

Alex stared up at the vent but couldn't tell if it was on or not. The vent was over ten feet up the wall and the room had nothing he could climb on to get up to that height.

He had a thought. When they had been laying out the room, Alex remembered that there were the two vents bringing in fresh air, but there was also one outtake vent to keep the air in motion, thus always having a continual flow of fresh air coming in as the stale air was forced out.

Alex went to the back of the room and saw the outtake vent with its black mesh cover making it look like a speaker. He ran over to the pile of supplies and grabbed a roll of toilet paper. He tore a thin strip and held it against the vent. If the system was working. The paper would be held against the vent gill as stale air was sucked out of the room.

The piece of paper hung limply in his hand. It wasn't sticking to the vent.

The air was off.

Alex knew that there was only so much breathable air that the room could hold. He had no idea how much the theatre held nor how long it would take to use it all up. He assumed that as it was a good-sized space, it should take a while. It just would have been nice to know exactly what 'a while' meant.

As Alex was trying to work out his oxygen dilemma, another problem occurred to him. He realised that he had to pee. His oxygen predicament had occupied all his thought processes, but now the urge to urinate was growing. The room design had included a couple of black matte metal waste bins that would have blended in with the room décor, but Alex had quashed that idea immediately. He thought they looked tacky and out of place.

Shame, Alex realised. They would have made great urinals. He wandered back to the supply collection and eyed the plastic bottles of water. They were big enough to hold a good quantity of piss, but they were currently full of water. Alex considered pouring out the liquid to make room for his own but couldn't bear to intentionally soak the custom carpet. One square yard had cost more than most people spend to re-carpet their entire house.

It then came to him that if he drank the bottle of water, the vessel would be empty and ready for filling. Alex also knew that he would be in effect creating a perpetual urinary cycle, but considering the alternative, decided that he didn't care.

He reached for the first bottle.

214

30

CHAPTER

By the time his car was returned by the valet, Aaron was furious. He had just attempted to formally launch the new Alex Cole and it couldn't have gone any worse. He'd been ignored, played, then punched. Where were all the adoring fans he'd expected to welcome him with open arms?

Aaron drove along Ventura until he reached the 405 freeway. He headed south until the Sunset Blvd turnoff, then drove between the dark shadowy hills of Bel Air on his left and the mainly unlit UCLA campus on his right.

Eight minutes later, he pulled up at Cindy's gate. He pressed the intercom button hoping that she wasn't going to give him any shit about being let in. He needn't have worried. The gate slide back without any verbal exchange.

As he pulled the Aston Martin up to the front of her house, he saw that she was standing outside waiting for him. That, however, was where the fantasy ended. She was wearing a pair of worn grey sweats. She seemed to have a black bandana covering her hair and had a pair of very unflattering glasses perched on the end of her nose.

With the whole dressed down thing, plus the fact that she hadn't put on a lick of makeup, to Aaron, she appeared exceedingly average.

This was not how Aaron had dreamed she would look at this momentous and life-changing moment in their lives.

"I thought you never drove that thing?" Cindy asked, nodding towards the Aston Martin.

"I thought I would as this is a special occasion," he replied as he stepped up towards her.

Aaron leaned in for a kiss, but she didn't notice and turned away and headed into the house.

"Come in and say whatever it is that's so damned important," Cindy said without even turning to face him. "I've got to be in makeup in five hours so make it quick."

Aaron closed the front door after him. He was starting to get angry. How dare she treat him like some studio assistant?! He had come all this way to let her know how he really felt about her. This wasn't something that could be done quickly. This was a speech that had been planned for over twenty years. He wasn't going to be rushed.

Cindy led him into a comfortable den at the back of the house. Dark, forest green walls framed the bright white fabric furniture.

"Fix yourself a drink if you want," she suggested.

Aaron realised that he was supposed to know where the booze was kept as he'd obviously been to the house many times before.

"Actually, I'll have a ginger ale to keep you company," Cindy said as she walked to a dark wood bookcase and pulled it towards her. It glided into the room then folded back against the wall revealing a hidden bar.

Cindy retrieved a single bottle of Canada Dry from a mini-fridge.

"Help yourself," she said as she flopped down on an oversized armchair.

Aaron poured himself an enormous highball glass of Armagnac then dumped a couple of ice cubes into it.

"Are you feeling alright?" Cindy asked. "Since when do you put ice in my best brandy?"

"There's a lot about me that you don't know," he replied, trying to sound suave and seductive.

"You know full well that there's nothing about you I don't know. So, come on… you've kept me up. Let's hear this earth-shattering speech."

Aaron took a long pull at his drink, feeling the amber liquid briefly warm his throat. He knew exactly what to say. He'd said it to himself a thousand times.

"Look, Cindy," he began. "I've known you for…"

The words froze in Aaron's throat as another woman entered the den. Tina Kent was in her mid-thirties, strongly built, with short black hair. She was wearing nothing but panties beneath a thin revealing robe.

She walked in front of Aaron without even acknowledging him. She sat on the arm of the chair Cindy was in and placed her hand affectionately on Cindy's shoulder.

"Has he told you what was so important?" Tina asked. Her voice was slightly raspy as if she was a long-time smoker.

"Who the hell are you?" Aaron blurted out.

"What are you talking about?" Cindy replied, surprised. "You've met Tina at least a hundred times."

"Are you a guest here?" Aaron asked Tina.

"If you call three and a half years a guest, then yeah. I guess I am," Tina replied before leaning down and kissing Cindy once, gently on the mouth.

"What the fuck is going on?" Aaron exploded. "This is all wrong. Everything about this is wrong. None of this is what I imagined."

"Alex, what the fuck are you talking about?" Cindy snapped at him. "What's wrong with what?"

"You... the way you look... the clothes... and... and... what's with the fucking rug muncher?" he babbled.

Tina got to her feet and took a step towards Aaron. Before he could even react, she punched him once in the solar plexus. He doubled over for the second time that night and dropped to his knees.

"I don't know what caveman bullshit you're channelling, but don't come into our house and talk to us like that," Tina seethed. "I don't care how big and famous you think you are, Alex, but behaviour like that isn't acceptable here."

Cindy slowly got to her feet.

"That's not Alex," she stated bluntly.

"What do you mean, he's not Alex?" Tina sounded confused.

Aaron suddenly sprang to his feet and charged at Tina with his arm out in front of him.

As Aaron didn't know who Tina was, he had no idea that she had been Cindy's stunt double for ten years before their secret civil ceremony three years earlier.

Her specialty was martial arts.

Tina side-stepped his arms then dropped and did a perfect sweeping kick that knocked Aaron's legs out from under him. He crumpled in a pile against one of the patio doors.

"Stay down, Alex, or whoever you are. If you try to get up, I'm going to have to really hurt you," Tina said calmly. "What do you mean, he's not Alex?" she asked Cindy.

"It's some guy they hired to be a double for Alex in public until the guy who shot him is arrested."

Aaron started to rise.

"I mean it," Tina said, "Don't get up."

Aaron held out his right hand and triggered his six-inch flick knife blade. He waved it back and forth in front of her as he carefully got to his feet.

"This was meant to be a special night for us," Aaron cried.

"I don't know about anyone else, but it's certainly been special for me," Tina commented.

"Shut up, you dyke. I wasn't talking to you," Aaron shouted.

"I had everything planned. I came over here to tell you how much I'd always loved you and you were supposed to say the same to me."

Tina tried to move slightly closer to Aaron. He sliced the air between them.

"Cindy… you and I together was always going to happen. I just knew it. I just knew that if you realised how I felt about you, it would all suddenly make sense. Cindy and Alex Cole together would have been the ultimate Hollywood royal family."

"What's your name?" Cindy asked gently. "I know Alex told me, but I forgot."

"I am Alex," Aaron replied. "That's what I'm trying to tell you. I've always been Alex."

"Okay… Alex. I think it's really sweet of you to think that way about me, but we can't be together. You can see that now, right?"

"See what? There's nothing stopping us now. I saw how you looked at me in *Days and Nights*. I saw how you kissed me. We should have been together back then, but it doesn't matter. We're together now."

Aaron stepped towards Cindy. Tina tried to kick his knife hand, but he somehow sensed her move. He swung the blade and managed to stab her in the thigh. He was about to bring down the knife again when Cindy grabbed his wrist.

"Don't hurt her. I can't be with you if you hurt my friends," Cindy whispered seductively.

Aaron turned and looked into her eyes.

"You mean…?" Aaron felt his heart soar.

"Yes, my darling," Cindy said as she seemed about to kiss him.

Aaron leant down and started to part his lips when the crystal vase smashed into the back of his head. Tina, blood oozing from her leg wound, dropped the shattered vase base and shoved him hard. He staggered and dropped to the ground.

The pain was excruciating. The flash of light that had filled his consciousness when the vase connected with his skull had gone, but Aaron was now feeling nauseous and dizzy and couldn't seem to focus his left eye. Thankfully, the vase hadn't been that heavy and had shattered immediately on contact. He felt the back of his head and winced. The wound was wet with blood. Pieces of crystal seemed to be imbedded in his scalp.

He still had the knife in his other hand and slowly got to his feet.

He no longer felt any love for Cindy.

All he felt now was the same as when those cheap whores had laughed at him back in Naples. He'd wanted to kill them. Now, he wanted to do the same to Cindy and her butch lover. He took a step towards them then heard a strange, soft thudding sound.

Something was rising up in the corner of his good eye.

Buster was a rescue dog. He'd been abandoned when his owner, a gang member in South Central, was shot by one of his own crew by mistake in a drive-by. Before that night, Buster had been trained by the punk to attack anyone who threatened him. Though now homed in a loving and nurturing household, Buster never fully forgot his training.

The 112-pound dog sank his teeth into Aaron's shoulder and let his weight lay the man out on the floor. Buster then stood back awaiting the next command.

Aaron somehow got to his feet. The knife had ended up under the coffee table. Aaron considered trying to grab it but knew the dog would probably go for his arm.

Buster growled menacingly. Cindy took him by the collar.

Though his mind was a mass of pain and confusion, Aaron knew that he had to get out of there. He stumbled towards the front door.

Buster tried to go after him but Cindy kept a firm hold.

"Sit," she commanded.

Buster sat.

31

CHAPTER

Aaron knew two things for certain. One was that he was hurt. The other was that he needed to get out of Los Angeles, immediately. He had no doubt that Cindy or her carpet muncher friend were going to call the police. He suddenly wondered why he'd chosen such a recognisable car from Alex's selection. Cindy had seen the Aston Martin when he'd arrived, and its description had almost certainly been passed onto every patrol car in the city.

Instead of driving down the hill away from her house, Aaron drove further up the winding streets. He was looking for something specific. He didn't yet know what, only that he'd know it the moment he saw it.

A few minutes later, he spotted what he was looking for. An old Nissan Sentra was parked in front of a 1960's-style Hawaiian bungalow on Loma Vista Drive. He switched off the Aston Martin's throaty V8 and coasted to the curb.

He'd never actually stolen a car before but he'd often helped stranded hotel guests who'd lost their keys or locked them in their car. He managed to break into the Nissan in less than a minute and had the engine going soon after that.

It felt like a piece of crap after driving the Aston, but all he needed was transport that wouldn't attract any attention. He had to get as far away as possible. He couldn't dare go to the West Hollywood house. That would be the first place they'd look. It suddenly dawned on him that he had no choice but to get back to Villa Miranda.

Aaron sighed as he realised that by returning to Alex's house, he would have no choice but to kill him, if he hadn't already run out of air. He tried to conceive of any reason why he should keep him alive. He tried to weigh the pros and cons of killing him immediately or not. His brain hurt as he tried to plan out the next move of a chess game that had stopped making any sense hours, if not years, earlier.

Whatever he needed to do, it had to happen in Montecito.

He had a quick look in the glove compartment and found a cheap woman's scarf. He tied it around his head, partly to staunch the oozing blood and maybe even ease some of the throbbing, but the main reason was to give him the appearance of being some poor female worker heading home in the middle of the night.

Aaron found his way to Coldwater Canyon and turned north. He crossed Mulholland then began the descent into the San Fernando Valley. The millions of lights that spread out in perfect geometric order were hypnotic. They seemed to twinkle as the illumination was warped by temperature changes in the air.

It almost made the valley seem appealing.

Aaron felt his head through the scarf and noticed that the blood flow hadn't abated at all. He wondered if the dizziness he was still feeling was because of blood loss or the initial blow. Whatever the reason, it didn't make driving at night any easier.

He was about to pull onto the 101 freeway when it dawned on him that choosing such a direct route might just be a poor decision considering the situation. Instead, he took surface streets to the 405 Freeway, then headed north to where it merged with the 5. He reached the town of Valencia with its fake-aged building facades and planned cookie-cutter communities.

Aaron shivered, not just because of the hopelessness and size of the sprawl, but because he was on the edge of going into shock. He pulled to the side of the freeway and closed his eyes while he tried to take some deep breaths to calm his heart. Almost immediately, he felt the claws of sleep begin to drag him into its dark warren.

Aaron snapped his eyes open and managed to re-join the traffic. A few miles later, he turned onto Highway 126 which was a straight run to Ventura, back on the coast. Other than the bizarre outdoor train museum that dominated the small town of Fillmore, he saw no other signs of life for the entire drive.

The thoughts of what had gone wrong began to ferment in his addled brain.

He'd never once considered the possibility that he would not become Alex Cole. By this point, his new life should have been well on the way to being focused on screwing Cindy, making movies and spending the millions he would be making from them.

Strangely, despite the years of detailed planning, Aaron never once considered that he wouldn't be accepted by the world as being the real Alex Cole. Little things like his eyes being the wrong colour and his fingerprints doubtless having entirely different swirl patterns, never worried him for a second. He never would have imagined that his meticulous and detailed scheme would have come so badly off the rails.

He blamed Cindy. She had always been the nucleus of his imagined new life. It was never just going to be him. It was going to be them. The one thing that he had never theorised was that Cindy was nothing like she was supposed to be.

Forget the fact that she preferred cunt over cock; it was her entire personality. The Cindy that he fell for all those years ago was fun-loving and sweetly romantic. He had envisioned her as a delightfully malleable girl who would follow his lead and instructions to the letter. Why else would he have become so besotted with her?

Who the hell would ever want some headstrong, opinionated shrew?

Aaron finally reached the town of Ventura then joined the 101 north, heading to Montecito and what he hoped would be, at least for a while, a safe haven. As he settled in for the final segment of his drive, a sharp stabbing pain enveloped his head. His vision blurred and he was forced to cut across three lanes of traffic so that he could pull over onto the hard shoulder.

Tears were flowing down his face as the pain seemed to somehow get worse. He removed the blood-soaked scarf and gingerly felt around the wound. He delicately touched each imbedded shard lightly with his index finger. The first two hurt like hell but that was to be expected. The third one was the prize winner. Even the gentlest of touches sent a bolt of sizzling electric pain through his body.

Everything went dark.

Aaron had no idea how long he'd been out, but as he floated back to some degree of consciousness, he knew that had to get off the hard shoulder and keep going. His left eye was no longer just a little blurry. He could hardly see a thing through it. What was even worse was that the nausea was back with a vengeance. As the old Nissan started to move, Aaron slammed on the brakes, pushed open the driver's door and puked violently onto the macadam.

Strangely, he felt better. Not ready to hike the Andes, but good enough, he hoped, to drive the final twenty-five miles home. Aaron found it strangely comforting that he was already considering Villa Miranda to be his home.

He reached the turn off twenty minutes later and headed up the hill. He hoped that the paparazzi vultures would have gone home by then. Aaron glanced at the cheap digital car clock and saw that it was 3:47. He had thought it was much later. He rounded the last bend before reaching his gate and saw that not only hadn't the media vacated their predatory positions but there was now a large police presence both outside the gate and on the driveway itself.

He couldn't understand how that was even possible, then spotted the reason. Diana-fucking-Trent was at the gate talking to two officers as she gestured angrily with her arms.

Aaron slowed the car and turned off the headlights. He let the Nissan coast backwards around the curve until he was completely out of sight from those gathered at his house. He desperately wanted to scream at the top of his lungs but knew that not only could he end up being heard, but such an action would doubtless end up being extremely painful to his already fragile head.

He put the car in gear then did a U-turn in the road. He knew that he needed to get away but couldn't think where to go to be safe. He just needed a base for a few days, just for long enough to find a way to blend in and become invisible among the unwashed masses of American society.

Aaron started to smile as an idea formed within his wounded head. He came up with the perfect plan. It was a good one too. He needed a place to hide out and only a few minutes away was ninety feet of sleek, fast, floating luxury.

He followed the circuitous route that Toni had used when Aaron had first arrived in California and was introduced to Alex's yacht. He found his way to the Santa Barbara harbour then followed the signs to the marina. He had no idea which basin they'd been in that night, only that it was where the larger boats were moored.

It only took a few minutes to find the security gate to Lucky Dancer's slip. Aaron stared at the push-button security lock expecting his usually sharp memory recall to retrieve the number that he'd seen Toni enter the last time he'd been there. Nothing came to him. He tried the keys on Alex's ring in case one of them would fit the gate but without success. He tried again to recall the number, but it just wouldn't float to the surface. He didn't know if it was the head injury or the shock, but he was drawing a complete blank. He gave his brain another few minutes to draw data from the recently cached files, but nothing came forward. It was as if there was blank space in his head where information used to be housed, but for some reason, simply wasn't there anymore.

He could see the dark outline of Lucky Dancer at the end of the jetty and knew that she was his only hope at that point. He was sure that if he could just get clear of the breakwater, he could go anywhere in that boat until it was time to covertly return to the real world.

Aaron was about to try and climb the security gate when a light clicked on behind him.

"What are you doing here?" a gruff voice asked.

Aaron turned and came face to face with a uniformed security guard. He was overweight and looked uncomfortable in his cheap Santa Barbara Marina Security uniform. A tarnished name tag read simply, BILL, as if his employers were too cheap to even fork out for the last name to be added.

"Oh heck," Bill stuttered. "I didn't know it was you, Mr. Cole. Is everything alright?"

"Everything's fine… Bill. I thought I'd come down to the boat for the night and just enjoy the quiet."

Bill noticed the blood that had seeped down onto Aaron's shoulders as well as the fact that he was as pale as one of those zombies he loved to watch on *The Walking Dead*.

"You look like you've been hurt," Bill said with real concern.

Aaron laughed and wiped his hand across the back of his head. The pain was explosive, but he managed to force a believable laugh.

"Oh hell," Aaron rolled his eyes. "I forgot to clean this stuff off. The studio sent a makeup artist to the house earlier today so we could do some tests for a head wound that I receive in my next film. I guess by looking at your face, she must have done a good job."

"Heck, yes," Bill nodded excitedly. "That could fool a battlefield medic."

"In my rush to get down here, I completely forgot my phone which has the gate code," Aaron said. "Would you mind, Bill?"

"Of course. I'd be delighted," Bill replied.

Instead of moving towards the gate, Bill looked down nervously at his feet.

"I will probably get into a heap of trouble for doing this…" Bill began.

Aaron thought for a moment that Bill had second thoughts about helping him. He wondered if, in his weakened state, he could still put the rent-a-cop down. He was bound to have a master pass key or fob that he could use to…

"Would it be possible for you to give me an autograph?" Bill asked. "I know that's inappropriate for an employee of the harbour to ask, but my wife would simply die if I came home with a note from Alex Cole to her."

Aaron felt relief flood through his body.

"That would be a pleasure, Bill. Do you have any paper?"

Bill frantically patted his polyester pockets until he located what looked to be a folded piece of copy paper. He handed it to Aaron together with a cheap Bic pen. With nowhere to rest the piece of paper, he gestured for Bill to turn the other way so he could use his back as a writing surface.

Bill turned away and smiled. He could already imagine the look on Glenda's face when he gave her a personalised note from her favourite movie star.

Aaron wrote, 'TO MY GOOD FRIEND BILL. PLEASE SAY HI TO YOUR BEAUTIFUL WIFE...'

"What's your wife's name?" Aaron asked.

"Glenda," he replied.

Aaron was about to finish the note when something about the piece of paper caught his eye. He unfolded it and saw that it was a printed copy of a police warning notification. The photo of Aaron was as clear as the text beneath it:

IF YOU SEE THIS MAN, PLEASE CALL 911 IMMEDIATELY. DO NOT APPROACH. SUSPECT IS BELIEVED TO BE ARMED AND DANGEROUS.

"Oh shit, Bill," Aaron sighed.

32

CHAPTER

Alex could tell that his breathing was becoming more laboured. He would take in a deep breath, but it seemed to not satisfy his body's need for oxygen. He'd tried taking lots of short breaths thinking that by doing that he was somehow getting more into his system, but all that had done was make him feel lightheaded. It also dawned on him that just maybe his continual pacing in the room was using up more oxygen than was really necessary.

The other problem was that the basement was getting hotter by the minute. He'd taken off his shirt earlier but was still sweating like a pig. It didn't help that he was drinking more water which meant more peeing which, in turn, required more water to be consumed to free up another bottle.

What a stupid situation to be in. He was glad that none of his fans could see him in this condition. He knew that there was nothing remotely heroic about being locked in a basement while slowly suffocating. In any of his films, Alex would have found a way to blow a hole in one of the walls or burrow out through the floor.

All he was doing was pacing in circles and pissing into plastic bottles.

It took a surprisingly long time of searching Bill's pockets before Aaron could find the small, brown, plastic key fob. Aaron waved it across the black IR reader and the security gate clicked open. As he approached the yacht, he saw that the vaguest hint of dawn's first glow was creeping up behind the Santa Barbara hills.

He knew he needed to be out of the harbour and preferably a good few miles offshore before it got much lighter. Aaron climbed the companionway and boarded the massive sports fisher. Thankfully, one of Alex's keys unlocked the aft door. Once inside, Aaron recognised exactly where Alex kept his set of boat keys. They were in a decoratively carved wooden box on the coffee table in the main salon.

Aaron went out on deck and climbed up the stainless steel steps to the flybridge. He sat at the outside helm and inserted the key.

Aaron wasn't a religious man, but he said a little prayer that the engines would start. If they didn't, he hadn't a clue what to do next.

He turned the master key then pushed the start button for the port engine. Even as he heard the diesel start to crank, he remembered that he hadn't vented the engine compartment.

He hoped that not doing so wouldn't be that big a deal.

The first explosion blew the aft deck more than fifty feet into the air sending fragments of teak and fibreglass raining down over the entire boat.

Aaron just had time to be relieved that the blast hadn't somehow reached the flybridge when the ruptured fuel tanks exploded sending a fireball right through the yacht's superstructure.

Aaron never felt a thing.

Marc Ciniatta and Tito Haniero were just pushing their fishing boat away from their slip as the sky flashed brilliant white, seconds before the shock wave of the first explosion reached them.

"What the hell was…" Marc called out.

The second flash was even brighter and the force of the blast knocked both men to the deck. As they got to their feet, they could see the fire raging on one of the big boats in the private marina. Tito grabbed the wheel and steered their thirty-foot Grady White towards a floating pile of burning debris.

"Nobody could have survived that," Marc shouted.

"We don't know that. We have to look," Tito called back.

As they moved slowly through the flaming remains of Lucky Dancer, Marc thought he saw something in the water.

"Stop. There's something over there," Marc pointed.

Tito angled the bow slightly to port as Marc grabbed a boat hook. There was something floating next to them that didn't look like debris. He grabbed their hand-held searchlight and pointed it toward the six-foot-long object.

Marc managed to snag the side of it and pull it closer. With the light shining straight down he could see that it was a body. A dead one. Whoever it had been was partially naked where the explosion had torn off his clothes. What skin was exposed was severely burned. Horrible gashes were visible all over the corpse.

Tito stopped the boat and joined his friend at the gunwale and looked down at the illuminated face.

"He's dead, man," he stated. "What do we do? Drag him on board?"

"I don't know," Marc replied.

While trying to decide their next move, the corpse's eyes opened.

Both men screamed.

Emergency responders were already nearing the site of the explosion when they were notified that a small craft had just found a man in the water. He was apparently in bad shape. Paramedics met the fishing boat at the nearest jetty and helped get the man into an ambulance, then remained with him for the short drive to Bayside Hospital.

As they brought him directly to the ER, Doctor Peter Eisner ran alongside listening to the report from the accompanying paramedics. They wheeled him into a curtained bay as the doctors and nurses began to work on the ravaged body.

One of the nurses, who was carrying out the trauma examination to gauge the degree of burn damage, found that much of what had been thought of as charred flesh on his face was actually a mix of smoke and oil. She cleaned off as much of as possible as the others evaluated the rest of the burns and wounds.

"I'm not sure where to start," Dr Eisner stated. "There's massive blood loss and at least forty percent burn coverage, mostly third degree. The issue is going to be infection from either the wounds or the burns. Floating around in that harbour water did him no favours. Do a cross match and prepare an Amoxiclav push. Hopefully, that will slow down the infection."

A nurse was about to draw blood for the cross-typing when Dr Eisner noticed the patient's face.

"Stop," he said. "I know who this is. He's already my patient. Look up Alex Cole, admitted within the two or three weeks, with me as attending. We did a cross-match at the time. That'll save a few minutes."

The nurse stepped over to a terminal and did a quick search.

"He's A positive," she called out.

"Start him on two units and have a third as back-up," he replied. "Where's that antibiotic push?"

Only a few miles away at Villa Miranda, the police and the media had left the property the second the explosion bloomed up into the night sky from the harbour. Alex Cole and Aaron Peterson's current locations became a secondary consideration. An explosion was much more interesting than even a missing film star.

It was always about the optics.

Diana was alone in the house, having decided to sleep there while waiting for some news about Alex's whereabouts. She probably should have been worried about Aaron as well, especially after what Cindy had told her, but from her description of the beating he'd taken, she doubted he'd be stupid enough to come back to the villa.

She was woken out of a light sleep by a loud knock on the front door. She mentally kicked herself for not having closed the front gates when the crowd had dispersed late the previous night.

"Who is it?" she shouted.

"It's Codi. let me in."

Diana threw open the door, smiled with relief and warmly embraced him.

"I thought you were in Tokyo?" Diana asked.

"I was but when I heard about Linda, I took the next plane out," Codi replied. "The moment I landed, I heard something about an attack on Cindy. There weren't many details."

"Yeah, it's been a laugh a minute on this side of the Pacific."

Diana led Codi to the living room then dropped onto the couch nearest the windows. Codi sat facing her.

"Where's Alex? I've been trying to call him."

"Nobody seems to know," Diana advised. "We do know, however, that when Aaron visited Cindy Snow's house and was acting crazy, he ended up stabbing Tina in the leg."

"For God's sake, why?" he asked, shocked.

"I haven't been able to talk directly to Cindy yet, but from what I gather, Aaron, pretending to be Alex, turned up drunk and started to profess his undying love for her, at which point things went pretty crazy," Diana explained.

"Understandably. Where's Aaron now?"

Diana shook her head. "He's missing as well."

"What the hell's going on?" Codi shook his head. "This is crazy."

"Did you hear about Larry Fritt?" Diana asked.

"No. What about him?" Codi replied.

"He's dead," Diana advised. "They arrested Toni Gonzales for his murder."

"Maria's Toni? No way. Not possible. How the hell Is Toni supposed to have killed him? No, back up. Why was he supposed to have killed him? They hardly knew each other."

"I know. It's obviously a mistake, but I feel so sorry for Toni and Maria."

"Let me know if I can help," Codi offered.

"Coffee?" Diana asked.

"That would be great," he replied.

"Make me one as well while you're up," Diana grinned back at him.

"I can't believe I fell for that again," Codi said as he got to his feet.

He made a cafetière of French roast then filled two mugs with the steaming brew. He returned to the living room and placed Diana's in front of her.

"What the hell is that?" Diana asked.

"Coffee," Codi replied.

"Not the drink. The vibration. Can't you feel it?"

Codi placed his mug on the table and sat completely still.

"I don't feel anything," he said.

"It's stopped," Diana said.

"Probably a helicopter somewhere overhead," Codi suggested.

As he reached for his mug, he saw the liquid suddenly shimmer.

"Feel it now?" Diana asked.

"I'm not just feeling it. I'm looking at it.

Diana followed his gaze. The coffee was rhythmically shuddering, sending little ripples to the side of the mug.

"Does Alex keep a herd of elephants in the house?" she asked with a straight face.

"Not exactly." Codi stood up and walked out of the room without a word. Diana jumped up and followed him. He walked to the main hallway and opened the oak door that shielded the inner entrance to the theatre/panic room. He put his palm against the cold steel then smiled. Diana looked confused.

"It's coming from the theatre," she stated. "You don't think…?"

"Open it and let's find out," Codi suggested.

"I don't have the passcode. Do you?"

"No. I never thought I'd need it," Codi replied.

"Maybe it's the same as the house code?" she suggested.

"Try it." Codi stood back to give her room to access the control panel.

Diana entered the code, but nothing happened. She looked crestfallen. She looked at Codi who was desperately trying to think of what else it could be. A smile started to form on his lips.

"Try Miranda's birthdate," he suggested.

Diana nodded her head in agreement. She entered the eight-digit number and the door slid open. They were immediately assaulted by the sound of *Jurassic Park* being played at an impossible volume. The subwoofers were in overdrive sending vibrations through the room and up through the rest of the house.

At the same moment as they reached Alex, stretched out on the floor with his eyes closed, Dr Eisner and the other emergency room team were trying desperately to resuscitate the man they thought was Alex Cole.

Almost as soon as they'd started the transfusion and broad-spectrum antibiotic drip, he'd started to shiver violently. Blisters and welts began to appear on his body and his breathing became raspy and forced.

After a further ten minutes, they stopped trying to revive him.

He was gone.

Dr Eisner called it at 07:12. As he was filling out the required forms, a nurse handed him a sheet of paper. His mouth dropped open as he read the post-mortem blood-type cross-check. It listed the man's blood type as being B negative. The nurse's report showed that once deceased, they'd drawn blood, but it couldn't be definitively typed. It was as if multiple blood groups were all mixed together. One of the nurses had the clever idea of typing the blood that had saturated the bandaging before the transfusion had taken place.

The result was clear and definitive. It was type B.

They'd given him two units of the wrong blood. Eisner knew that was impossible. He had verified the cross-check when Alex had come in with his leg injury.

He got to his feet and approached the shrouded body. Dr Eisner pulled back the surgical sheet, exposing the man's legs. He examined every inch of the corpse's right leg for any sight of the stitches and subsequent scar. There was no trace of the injury. Feeling as if someone had tilted his entire world, Eisner checked the other leg as well.

He sat back down and placed his head in his hands. He knew that the whoever it was that he'd just treated had been unlikely to survive, but by giving him the wrong blood, Eisner had sealed the deal.

33

CHAPTER

Paramedics finished examining Alex and pronounced him a little dehydrated but otherwise in decent shape. They felt that the headache, nausea and dizziness were almost certainly the results of a combination of the air having been shut off to the room and the blow to the head. There was no sign of concussion or any other symptom that required hospitalisation.

While he was being examined, a detective from the SBPD took down Alex's statement about his earlier interaction with Aaron, including his plans to kill many others.

Alex looked smaller than usual and a bit frail as he sat in one of the plush cinema seats.

"Thank you for finding me," he said to Diana.

"Looks like we were just in time." Codi gestured with his head towards the six urine-filled plastic bottles. "Looks like you were having a little Howard Hughes moment down here on your own."

"You should thank Codi," she replied, trying to suppress a laugh. "I'm not sure how long it would have taken me to figure out that the vibration in the house was due to the subwoofers."

"It was your joke about the elephants that pointed me to the theatre," Codi conceded.

"The T-Rex demo," Alex sighed.

"What T-Rex demo?" Diana asked.

"It's not something we're proud of but when Dolby installed the system, they used the first T-Rex scene from Jurassic Park as a demo to show us what the speakers could handle. The moment the installers were gone, Alex over there produced some exceptional weed and after ingesting a substantial amount of the wacky baccy, we sat down here for hours just watching and listening to that scene over and over again.

"The sound was extraordinary," Alex added.

"When we stumbled upstairs, Maria was standing in the hallway tapping her foot like an impatient parent. Apparently, the house had been vibrating the whole time, driving her and Toni crazy.

"Why didn't you play the damn scene sooner?" Diana scolded. "I could have had you out of there at least twelve hours earlier."

"That's assuming you would have figured out where the vibration was coming from," Codi reminded her. "It's kind of a guy thing."

He gave her one of his cheeky grins, so she knew he was joking. It didn't seem to matter. She punched him in the arm anyway. Hard.

"It wasn't Diana's fault," Alex said. "The fact is I only thought of it once the oxygen level started to get dangerously low. I started getting lightheaded and thought of that time we blasted the subs."

"Sorry to just walk in," Detective Morales said as she came down the theatre stairs. "I tried ringing, but nobody answered."

"The whole room is soundproofed," Alex volunteered.

"Glad to see that you're alive, Mr Cole," Morales said.

"That makes two of us," Alex replied with a weak smile.

"We found Aaron Peterson," she advised.

"Hopefully dead in a ditch somewhere," Diana voiced then realised she was being a little crass.

"Not a ditch," Morales responded. "He died in the Santa Barbara ER about an hour and a half ago."

"Jesus," Alex gasped. "What happened to him?"

The detective who took down Alex's statement interrupted and asked to speak with Morales in private. The two left the others alone in the basement for almost ten minutes. Only Detective Morales returned.

"First of all, Mr Cole, I feel I should offer you my condolences."

"That's very kind, Detective, but I don't consider the guy's death to be much of a tragedy." Alex shrugged.

"I was referring to your yacht, the Lucky Dancer," Morales replied. "I'm afraid that what's left of her is resting on the bottom of the marina."

"What?" Diana blurted out. "How the hell did that happen?"

With Diana and Codi listening with rapt attention, Detective Morales told them about the unconscious security guard, Aaron's attempt to steal the yacht and the subsequent explosion.

Alex and Codi turned to face each other.

"He didn't use the blowers," the two said in almost perfect unison.

"Two fishermen found his body floating almost a hundred feet from where the Lucky Dancer exploded," Morales explained. "Amazingly, he was still alive. They got him to Bayside Hospital, but he died in the ER."

"It must have been one hell of an explosion," Codi stated.

"It wasn't the blast that finally killed him. It appears that the attending doctor recognised him. It was the same doctor who treated you after your boat accident a few weeks ago. As he believed he was treating you, he knew your blood type and your allergies. Sadly, that data didn't even remotely match Aaron's medical records. They mistakenly administered antibiotics to someone who was highly allergic to them and then gave him the wrong blood type. All of this must be confirmed by autopsy, but after Aaron coded, Dr Eisner checked for the leg injury that you recently sustained.

"It wasn't there," Alex whispered.

"It was not," Morales confirmed.

"Are we to assume that Aaron is now the prime suspect, all be it posthumously, in Larry Fritt's murder?" Diana asked.

"Obviously, I can't give you any specifics about an ongoing investigation, but I can say that we will be reviewing the evidence in the case considering Mister Peterson's attack on Miss Holt and his kidnapping of you, Mister Cole. We did have one small breakthrough late yesterday. We managed to trace his financial history to a savings account that nobody seemed to know about. It was in a bank in Utah that he hardly ever used. The strange thing was that he received a monthly payment of $50,000 from an offshore bank in the Caymans. So far, we've had no luck in getting access to it or working out what the payments were for."

"That's odd," Diana commented.

"Isn't it?" Morales agreed. "Payments like that usually lead us to believe that blackmail is involved."

"You think Larry was a blackmailer?" Alex asked, shocked.

"It certainly looks that way, but unless the foreign bank suddenly develops a conscience, which I doubt will ever happen, we have no way of knowing who the money was coming from."

"What about his computer and that iPad he carried everywhere? Was there anything relevant on those?" Diana asked.

"Both are missing," Morales said. "We assume that the killer took them."

"If there any doubt that Aaron was the killer?" Diana asked.

"Everything points to him. Especially now that we know what Larry had found out in Florida. Aaron must have felt that he needed him silenced, so he definitely had the motive."

"Are you positive that Aaron was the one who shot me?" Alex asked.

"Obviously, as he confessed that to you before locking you down here, that investigation is now far more focused on him having been the sole perpetrator," Morales replied.

"What about the marina security guard?" Diana asked.

"He's got a nasty bump on his head and is being kept in the hospital for observation, but he seems to be okay," she advised.

"Diana, would you please contact the hospital and have the man moved to a private room," Alex instructed," Let them know that I will be paying all his medical costs."

"Aaron's as well?" Codi asked, tongue in cheek.

"Fuck that," Alex replied, not joking. "What about Toni?"

"I was just getting to that," the detective said. "When we searched your property with Ms Trent in attendance, we noticed exterior security cameras. Ms Trent gave us permission to access the cloud data from the system. On the night that Mr Fritt was murdered, Mr Gonzales was recorded over a dozen times on your property. The most important clips were of him wheeling out your trash for city collection the next day and then washing one of your cars in the driveway. The two clips were time-stamped and showed Mr Gonzales to have been on your property at the time when we believe Mr Fritt was attacked and killed."

"So, Toni's in the clear?" Alex asked.

"Between the video and Mister Peterson's confession to you about killing others, it seems pretty obvious that he was responsible," Morales acknowledged. "I believe your lawyer has been trying to call you to give you the news."

"I don't know where my phone is," Alex stated.

244

The ER bay where Aaron died was still in the process of being cleaned. There had been a lot of blood and charred flesh to remove. The deceased's personal belongings were in a large medical ziplock bag on a side prep table.

The cleaning and sterilisation technician was wiping down one of the stainless-steel treatment table legs when the room filled with the sound of *The Ride of the Valkyries*. He looked over to the prep table and saw a damaged iPhone vibrating within the plastic baggie.

After the third blast of Wagner's epic piece of music, the iPhone screen flickered twice then faded to black.

34

CHAPTER

Once the police had left, Codi headed back to LA so he could catch up on some badly needed sleep.

Alex was pouring himself a sizeable brandy when Diana walked into the living room.

"I thought you'd gone to bed," she said.

"I did, but I couldn't sleep," Alex replied.

"That's not surprising considering what's been going on for the last few days. I doubt I'll get any sleep either."

"That's not what's keeping me awake," he said.

"Oh. What is?"

Alex walked to the French doors at the end of the room and looked out into the darkness.

"It was something that Detective Morales said that's been bothering me," Alex said, downing half the glass of amber liquid. "She said that Larry had been receiving payments from a bank in the Cayman Islands."

"Yes, she did," Diana agreed.

"I visit there a lot," Alex stated.

"It's a beautiful island," she replied.

"I have a bank account in the Caymans," Alex continued.

"I know," Diana sighed. "I also know that you were being blackmailed."

"You were always the smart one, weren't you?" Alex said.

"I was smart enough to work out that someone was forcing you to pay out extortion money," Diana replied as Alex turned to face her. "What I didn't know was why."

"You don't want to know."

"I thought you knew me better than that," she said. "Of course, I want to know."

Alex took a moment to gather his thoughts and work out how to put them into words.

"When I was still in *Days and Nights,* I went to a lot of wild parties. One of them was at a house in the Hollywood Hills. There were so many drugs and so many beautiful girls."

"Oh, Alex. What did you do?"

"I still don't know how it happened but…there was this really cute girl… she swore that she was over eighteen. We pretended to check out the house and snuck off to one of the bedrooms. We messed around then she started slurring her words and passed out. I wasn't sure if she was breathing or not. I tried to sneak out of the room so I wouldn't be found with the girl when some rent-a-cop caught me. Turned out he wasn't a real policeman. He was private security from the studio. He managed to revive her and found out that she was fifteen. It cost me everything I had in the bank, but he managed to whitewash the whole thing. Everything. There was no trace of me anywhere and the girl never said a word."

"The security guy was Larry, wasn't it?" Diana asked.

Alex nodded. "Yeah. He had just left the force and started his own company. That night was his first job."

"Lucky for you," Diana commented.

"I thought so too until a couple of years ago when he dropped by the sound stage and told me that he'd taken pictures of the girl and had collected hair and fibre samples from the bed. Because of the whole *me too* movement, Larry felt that it was his duty to contact the victim, as he put it, and make sure that what happened to her became public knowledge. He pointed out that not only would my career be destroyed, but I was almost certain to do some prison time."

"And that's when he started blackmailing you?" she asked.

"Yup."

"And now he's dead," she stated.

Alex nodded. "I know I shouldn't think it, but Aaron did me a huge favour."

Diana laughed. "You really believe that?"

"Of course," Alex answered. "With him gone, I'm in the clear. It wasn't the money. It was the knowledge that he could destroy me at any time. Who would have thought that by hiring that nut job to cover for me, we would be saving me from something far more destructive?"

"Sounds like karma," she said.

"It does, doesn't it?" Alex said. "The problem is that whatever evidence Larry had against me is now most likely in the hands of the police."

Diana smiled.

"It's guaranteed to leak out now," Alex said, shaking his head. "That'll be the end of me. It'll be like Polanski, except I can't flee the country. You'd better start distancing yourself from me. You don't want to be anywhere near when this shit hits the fan."

"What if Larry's proof was no longer an issue?" Diana asked.

"That would be a miracle, but unlikely. As soon as they locate his iPad and laptop, it's only a matter of time before they stumble across the evidence he collected."

"I think you'll find that the data on both devices has been corrupted," Diana advised. "It's amazing what you can do with a thumb drive nowadays. Besides, the photos and samples were locked in his desk drawer. They're now nothing but ash."

"Why would you…" Alex felt his legs turn to jelly.

"You?" he managed to ask.

Diana simply nodded.

"You killed him?"

"Somebody had to. The man was a pig. Did you know that at last year's Christmas party at your home, he tried to rape me in the guesthouse?"

"Did he…?" Alex stuttered.

"No, he did not. However, he did have to go to the emergency room with a crushed testicle."

"You did that?" he asked.

"You bet I did. He didn't seem to be understanding the word, no."

"Why did you kill him? I mean, you had good reason to; I guess I mean why did you kill him now?"

"I knew about the blackmail, and after his attack on me, I had a whole slew of crazy ideas floating around in my head, but it wasn't until Aaron started going off the deep end that I came up with the idea of killing two birds with one stone… so to speak."

"Why frame Toni?" Alex asked.

"I knew it wouldn't stick. I wanted it to look like something a sociopath would do…what Aaron would do."

"I don't know what to say," Alex replied.

"A simple thank you will suffice. I hope you know that I've always had your back."

"This is a little beyond simply having my back, isn't it?" Alex pointed out.

"Not really," Diana said. "That pig had the power to destroy you. I just decided to stop him, that's all."

"What makes you think I won't turn you in?" Alex asked.

"What makes you think I'd let you?" she said, smiling.

"So where do we go from here?"

"Where do you want us to go?" Diana said as she stepped close to him.

"I thought you didn't want to get involved that way?" Alex said.

"I didn't… then. Now, the dynamics have changed, haven't they?" she said as she looked deep into his eyes.

"You said that you could never have a relationship with the man who signed your pay-check."

"I know I did. That's why I'm giving you notice, effective immediately."

"Are you serious?" Alex asked.

"I just killed a man for you. How fucking serious do I have to be?"

"Are sure about this?"

"You know I've always loved you, don't you?" Diana said in little more than a whisper.

"Yes. And I hope you know that I fell for you back in high school. There was something about the way you used to twirl your hair that drove me crazy."

"Then why didn't you let me know?" she asked.

"You were my best friend," Alex replied. "I didn't want to screw that up."

"What about now? Do you think best friends could be something more?"

Alex looked back into her eyes, then took her hand and started to lead her to his bedroom.

"I've never made love to a murderer before," Alex said.

"You'll get used to it," Diana replied as she gently punched his arm.

THE END